Larry.

Love from.

Aunty Edith & Uncle Herb.

Tiger By The Tail

and Other Science Fiction Stories

TIGER BY THE TAIL

and Other Science Fiction Stories

by ALAN E. NOURSE

DAVID McKAY COMPANY, INC. New York

Manufactured in the United States of America

Acknowledgments

The author and the publishers wish to thank the following for permission to reprint:

Galaxy Publishing Corporation, New York, N. Y.:

"Tiger by the Tail," copyright 1951 by Galaxy Publishing Corporation; "PRoblem" and "Brightside Crossing," copyright 1956 by Galaxy Publishing Corporation; and "The Coffin Cure," copyright 1957 by Galaxy Publishing Corporation. All reprinted from *Galaxy Magazine.*

Great American Publications, New York, N. Y.:

"The Native Soil," reprinted from *Fantastic Universe,* copyright 1957 by King-Size Publications, Inc.

Mercury Press, Inc., New York, N. Y.:

"Love Thy Vimp," reprinted from *The Magazine of Fantasy and Science Fiction.*

Quinn Publishing Company, Inc., Kingston, N. Y.:

"Letter of the Law," reprinted from *IF Magazine.*

Street & Smith Publications, Inc., New York, N. Y.:

"Nightmare Brother," and "Family Resemblance," copyright 1953 by Street & Smith Publications, Inc.; reprinted from *Astounding Science Fiction* (now known as *Analog Science Fact & Fiction*).

Contents

Tiger By The Tail

and Other Science Fiction Stories

Tiger By The Tail

THE department store was so crowded with the postseason rush, it was surprising that they spotted her at all. The salesgirl at the counter was busy at the far end, and the woman was equally busy at her own end, slipping goods from the counter into the large black purse. Kearney watched her in alarm for several minutes before calling over the other section manager.

"Look at that woman!" he said. "She's sorting that hardware like she owns the store."

"A klepto? What are we waiting for?" asked the other. "Let's have a talk with her."

Kearney scratched his head. "Watch her for a minute. There's something fishy—"

They watched. She was standing at the kitchenware counter, her hands running over the merchandise on the shelf. She took three cookie cutters and popped them into the pocketbook.

Two large cake tins and a potato masher followed, then a small cake safe, two small pots and a large aluminum skillet.

The second man stared in disbelief. "She's taken enough junk there to stock a store. And she's putting it all into that pocketbook. Kearney, *she couldn't get all that junk into a pocketbook!*"

"I know," said Kearney. "Let's go."

They moved in on her from opposite sides, and Kearney took her gently by the arm. "We'd like to speak to you, madam. Please come with us quietly."

She looked up blankly. "What do you mean?"

"We've been watching you load that pocketbook for fifteen minutes."

"Pocketbook?" the woman said, bewildered.

Kearney took the pocketbook from her arm, unsnapped it, glanced inside, and shook it in alarm.

He looked up, eyes wide and puzzled. "Jerry, *look at this.*"

Jerry looked. When he tried to speak, there just weren't any words.

The pocketbook was empty.

Frank Collins parked his car in front of the Institute of Physics and was passed by fingerprint into the lab wing. Evanson met him in the corridor.

"Glad you got here," Evanson said grimly.

"Listen, John, what *is* this about a pocketbook? I hope it's not your idea of a joke."

"Not this gadget," Evanson promised. "Wait till you see it."

He led the way into one of the large lab sections. Collins eyed the shiny control panels uneasily, the giant generators and boosters, the duocalc relay board with its gleaming tubes and confusion of wiring. "I can't see what you want with me here. I'm a mechanical engineer."

Evanson walked into a small office off the lab. "You're also a trouble shooter from way back. Meet the research team, Frank."

The research team wore smocks, glasses, and a slouch. Collins nodded, and looked at the pocketbook lying on the table.

"Looks just like any other pocketbook to me," he said. He picked it up. It felt like a pocketbook. "What's in it?"

"You tell us," Evanson said.

Collins opened it up. It was curiously dark inside, with a dull metallic ring around the opening, near the top. He turned it upside down and shook it. Nothing came out.

"Don't reach around inside," Evanson cautioned. "It's not safe. One fellow tried, and lost a wrist watch."

Collins looked up, his bland face curious. "Where did you get this?"

"A couple of section managers spotted a shoplifter down in the Taylor-Hyden store a few days ago. She was helping herself to kitchen hardware, and was stuffing her pocketbook full. They nabbed her, but when they tried to get the hardware back out of the pocketbook they couldn't find any. One of them lost a wrist watch groping around in it."

"Yes, but how did *you* wind up with the purse?"

Evanson shrugged. "They turned the woman over to Psych, naturally. She denied ever seeing the purse. And when the Psych boys looked at the pocketbook they called us in a hurry. Here, I'll show you why."

Evanson picked up a meter stick and began to push it into the pocketbook. It went in about ten centimeters, to the bottom of the purse. . . .

And kept on going!

It didn't poke out the bottom. It didn't even bulge the purse.

Collins goggled at it. "Holy smoke, how'd you do that?"

"Maybe it's going somewhere else. Fourth dimension. I don't know."

"Nuts!"

"Where else, then?" Evanson laid the meter stick down. "Another thing about that pocketbook," he added, "no matter what you do, you *can't* turn it inside out."

Collins looked at the dark inside of the pocketbook. Gingerly he stuck his finger in, rubbed the metallic ring, scratched it with his nail. A shiny line appeared. "That's aluminum in there," he said. "An aluminum circle."

Evanson nodded, "All the stuff she was stealing was aluminum," he said. "That's one reason we called you. You're an engineer, and you know your metals. We've been trying for three days to figure out what's happening inside that purse. We still don't know. Maybe you can tell us."

"What have you been doing?"

"Pushing stuff into it. Checking it with all the instruments. X-ray, everything. Didn't tell us a thing. We'd like to know where that stuff that we push in goes."

Collins dropped an aluminum button into the purse. It went through the aluminum circle and vanished. "Say," he asked suddenly, scowling. "What do you mean, you can't turn this thing inside out?"

"It's a second-order geometric form." Evanson lit a cigarette carefully. "You can turn a first-order form, like a sphere or a rubber ball, inside out through a small hole in the surface. But you *can't* turn an inner tube inside out, no matter what you do."

"Hm. Why not?"

"Because it's got a hole in it. And you can't pull a hole through a hole. Not even an infinitesimal hole."

"So?" Collins said, frowning.

"So it's the same with that purse. We think it's wrapped around a chunk of another universe. A four-dimensional universe. And you can't pull a chunk of another universe through this one without causing a lot of trouble."

"But you *can* turn an inner tube inside out," Collins protested. "It may stretch all out of shape, but you can pull it through the hole."

Evanson eyed the pocketbook on the table. "Maybe so. A second-order geometric under conditions of stress. But there's one hitch to that. *It won't be an inner tube any more."*

He took another bit of aluminum and fed it into the purse. He shook his head tiredly. "I don't know. The stuff is going *somewhere."* He pushed a wooden ruler in, watched it pop right out again. "And it takes *only* aluminum. Nothing else. That detective had an aluminum military watch, which disappeared from his wrist, but he had two gold rings on the same hand, and neither one was touched."

"Let's play some thinking games," Collins said.

Evanson looked up sharply. "What do you mean?"

Collins grinned. *"Whatever* is on the other side of that pocketbook seems to want aluminum. Why? There's an aluminum ring around the mouth of the purse—all around it. Like a portal. But it isn't very big, and it doesn't use much aluminum. They seem to want lots more."

"They?"

"Whatever takes the metal but pushes back the wood."

"Why?"

"We could venture a guess. Maybe they're building *another* opening. A large one."

Evanson stared at him. "Don't be silly," he said. "Why—"

"I was just thinking out loud," said Collins mildly. He picked up the steel meter stick. Taking a firm grip on one end, he pushed the other end into the purse.

Evanson watched, puzzled. "They don't want it. They're trying to push it back."

Collins continued to push the stick in, perspiring a little. Suddenly the end appeared, curving back out. Like a flash Collins grabbed it and began tugging both ends at once.

"Watch it, watch it!" Evanson snapped. "You'll twist their universe to conform to our geometry!" The purse seemed to be sagging inward.

One end of the stick suddenly slipped out of Collins' hand. He fell back, pulling it out of the pocketbook. It was straight again.

Collins stared at it, and his eyes narrowed. "Can you get a winch up here?"

"I think so," Evanson said.

"Good," said Collins. "I think I know how we can hook onto their universe."

The big three-inch steel bar rolled easily into the lab on a dolly. The end of the bar was covered with shiny aluminum tubing and bent into a sharp hook.

"Is the winch ready?" Collins asked.

"All set," Evanson said.

"Then slide the purse onto the end of the bar."

The end of the bar disappeared into the pocketbook.

"What are you trying to do?" Evanson asked uneasily.

"They seem to want aluminum, so we're going to give them some. If they're building another opening through with it, I want to hook onto the opening and pull it out into this lab.

They'll be putting the aluminum on this bar with the rest. If we can hook onto what they already have, they'll either have to cut it free and let us retrieve it, or open it into this lab."

Evanson scowled. "But what if they don't do either?"

"They *have* to. If we pull a non-free section of their universe through the purse, it will put a terrific strain on their whole geometric pattern. Their whole universe will be twisted. Just like an inner tube."

The winch squeaked as Collins worked the bar to and fro inside the purse.

"Up a little," he said to the operator.

Evanson shook his head sourly. "I don't see—" he began. The bar twanged under sudden pressure.

"Hold it! You've got it hooked!" Collins shouted.

The winch squealed noisily, the motor whining under the strain. The steel bar began sliding slowly out of the purse, millimeter by millimeter. Every ten minutes one of the technicians made a chalk mark on the bar by the mouth of the purse.

Frank Collins filled a pipe and puffed nervously. "The way I see it," he said, "these beings pried a small fourth-dimension hole into our universe, and somehow got that woman under control. Then they made her start collecting aluminum so they could build a bigger opening."

"But why?" Evanson poured coffee out of a thermos. It was late, and the whole building was silent and deserted except for this one lab section. The only noise in the room was the whine of the winch, tugging away at the other universe.

"Who knows? To get more and more aluminum? Whatever the reason, they want to get through to our universe. Maybe theirs is in some kind of danger. The reason may be so alien that we couldn't possibly understand it."

"But what's the idea of hooking onto them?" Evanson's eyes were worried.

"Control. We pull a non-free chunk of their universe into ours, and they can't use the opening. It'll be plugged up. The more we pull through, the more strain on the structure of their universe. They'll have to listen to *our* terms then. They'll have to give us their information so that we can build openings and examine them properly. If they don't, we'll wreck their universe."

"But you don't even know what they're *doing* in there!"

Collins shrugged, made another chalk mark on the bar. The bar was humming under the strain.

"I don't think we should take the risk," Evanson complained. "I didn't have permission to try this. I just let you go ahead on my own authority, on data—" he shuddered suddenly— "that's so vague it makes no sense at all."

Collins knocked out his pipe sharply. "It's all the data we have."

"I say it's wrong. I think we should release the bar right now, and wait till Chalmers gets here in the morning."

Collins eyed the winch with growing uneasiness. His fingers trembled as he lit his pipe again. "Don't be foolish," he said. "We *can't* release the bar now. The tapered sheaves are under too much tension. We couldn't even burn through that rod with an oxy torch in less than twenty minutes—and it would jolt the whole building apart when it broke."

"But the danger—" Evanson stood up, his forehead beaded with perspiration. He nodded toward the creaking winch. "You might be gambling our whole universe."

"Oh, calm down!" Collins said angrily. "We don't have any choice now. We're *doing* it, and that's all there is to it. When you grab a tiger by the tail, you've got to hang on."

Evanson crossed the room excitedly. "It seems to me," he said tensely, "that the tiger might have the advantage. If it went the wrong way, think what *they* could do to *our* universe!"

Collins rubbed his chin nervously. "Well, at any rate, I'm glad we thought of it first—" He trailed off, his face slowly turning white.

Evanson followed his stare, and his breath came in a sharp gasp. The thermos clattered noisily to the floor. He pointed at the second chalk mark, sliding slowly *into* the pocketbook.

"You mean you hope we did," he said.

Nightmare Brother

HE was walking down a tunnel.

At first it didn't even occur to him to wonder *why* he he was walking down the tunnel, nor how he happened to be there, nor just what tunnel it was. He was walking quickly, with short, even steps, and it seemed as if he had been walking in the same direction for hours.

It wasn't the darkness that bothered him at first. The tunnel wasn't bright, but it was quite light enough, for the walls glowed faintly with a bluish luminescence. Ahead of him the glowing walls stretched as far as he could see. The tunnel was about ten feet wide, and ten feet high, with smooth walls arching into a perfectly smooth curve over his head. Under his feet the floor seemed cushiony, yielding slightly to the pressure as he walked, and giving off a soft, muffled sound in perfect measure to his tread. It was a pleasant, soothing sound; he had not paused at all to wonder just what he was doing there. It was quite obvious, after all. As simple as simple could be. He was walking down a tunnel.

But then a flicker of caution crept into his mind, and a frown crossed his quiet face. He stopped abruptly, peering around him at the glowing walls in growing confusion. What a very odd place to be, he thought. A tunnel! He turned his head, listening for a long moment, until the stark silence of the place made his skin prickle.

He sniffed audibly and scratched his head. My name is David Cox, he thought, and I am walking down a tunnel. He pondered for a moment, trying to remember. How long had he been walking? An hour? He shook his head. It must have been longer than that. Oddly, he couldn't remember *when* he had started walking. But how had he gotten here? What had he been doing before he came into the tunnel? His alarm grew as his mind groped for answers that weren't there. What had happened to his memory? Little doors in his mind seemed to snap quickly shut even as he approached them. Ridiculous, he thought, to be walking down a tunnel without even knowing where it was leading—

He peered forward in the silence. He was absolutely alone; there was not a sound around him, not a stir, no sign of another human being, nor a flicker of life of any kind. The chill deepened, and he walked cautiously over to one wall, tapped it with his knuckles. Only a dull knock. He shrugged his shoulders then, and started on. After all, there was really no reason to be alarmed. A tunnel had to have an end, somewhere.

And then he heard the sound. It came to his ears very faintly, at first, the most curious sort of airy whistling, like a shrill pipe in the distance. It cut through the stillness like a razor. He listened, hardly breathing. Was the light growing fainter? Or were his eyes not behaving? He blinked, and sensed the light dimming even as the whistling sound grew louder and nearer, mingling with another, deeper sound. A throbbing roar came to his ears, blending with the shrillness of the whistle, and then he saw the light, far down the tunnel.

It was a single round, yellow light directly in the center of the passage ahead, growing larger and brighter as the roar intensified. A breeze brushed his cheek as he stared, fascinated by the yellow light bearing down on him. A horrible image crossed his mind, the image of a man trapped on a railroad track as a dark engine approached with whistle screaming, bearing down like some hideous monster out of the night—

A cry broke from his lips. *It was a train!* Roaring down the tunnel toward him, it was moving like a demon with no tracks, screeching its warning as it came, with the light growing brighter and brighter, blinding him. It came on relentlessly, filling the tunnel from side to side, hissing smoke and fire and steam from its valves, its whistle shrieking.

In panic David Cox threw himself face down on the floor, trying frantically to burrow deeper into the soft mat of the tunnel floor, closing his mind down, blanking out everything but horrible, blinding fear. The light blazed to floodlight brilliance; with a fearful rush of wind the roar increased to a sudden thundering bellow over his head. Then it gave way to the loud, metallic clak-clak-clak of steel wheels on steel rails beside his ears, and faded slowly into the distance behind him. . . .

Trembling uncontrollably in every muscle, Cox tried to rise to his knees, groping for control of his mind. His eyes were closed tightly, and suddenly the floor was no longer soft matting, but a gritty stuff that seemed to run through his fingers.

He opened his eyes with a start, and a cry came to his lips. The tunnel was gone. He was standing ankle-deep in the steaming sand of a vast, yellow desert, with a brassy sun beating down from a purple sky. He blinked, unbelieving, at the yellow dunes, and a twisted Joshua tree blinked back at him not ten feet away.

Two men and a girl stood in the room, watching the motionless body of the man sprawled on the bed. The late afternoon sun came in the window, throwing bright yellow panels across the white bedspread, but the man lay quite still, his pale eyes wide open and glassy, oblivious to anything in the room. His face was as white as the bedspread.

The girl gasped. "I think he's stopped breathing," she whispered.

The taller of the men, dressed in white, took her by the shoulder, gently turning her face away. "He's still breathing," he reassured her. "You shouldn't be here, Mary. You should go home, try to get some rest. He'll be all right."

The other man snorted, his pink face flushed with anger. "He shouldn't be here either," he hissed, jerking a thumb at the man on the bed. "I tell you, Paul, David Cox is not the man. I don't care what you say. He'll never get through."

Dr. Paul Schiml drew a deep breath, turning to face the other. "If Cox can't get through, there isn't a man in the Hoffman Medical Center who can—or ever will. You know that."

"I know that there were fifty others in the same training program who were better fitted for this than Dave Cox!"

"That's not true." Dr. Schiml's voice was sharp in the still room. "Reaction time, ingenuity, opportunism—not one in the group could hold a candle to Dave." He stared down at the red-faced man with contempt. "Admit it, Connover. You're not worried about Dave. You're worried for your own neck. You've been afraid since the start, since the first ships came back to Earth, because you've been in charge of a program you don't believe in, and you're afraid of what will happen if Dave Cox doesn't come through. It wouldn't matter who was on that bed, you'd still be afraid." He sniffed in disgust. "Well, you needn't worry. Dave Cox will do it, if anyone can. He *has* to."

"And if he doesn't?"

The tall doctor stared at Connover for a moment. Then he turned abruptly and walked over to the bedside. There was hardly a flicker of life in the man who lay there, only the shallowest respiration to indicate that he *was* alive. With gentle fingers Dr. Schiml inspected the small incision in the man's skull, checked again the multitude of tiny, glittering wires leading to the light panel by the bedside. He stopped, peering at the panel, and motioned sharply to Connover. "Here's the first, already," he whispered.

For a moment, only the faintest buzz of sound could be heard from the panel; then Connover let out a soft whistle. "A tunnel. That makes sense. But what a device—" He turned wide-eyed to Schiml. "He could kill himself!"

"Of course he could. We've known that from the start."

"But *he* doesn't know."

"He doesn't know anything." Schiml pointed to the panel. "A train. Ingenious? It's amazing. Could you think of anything worse?" He watched for a moment. "No room on either side for escape—he'll go under it."

All three watched, hardly breathing. Suddenly the girl was sobbing uncontrollably, burying her face on the doctor's shoulder. "It's horrible," she choked. "It's horrible—he'll never make it, never, he'll be killed."

"No, Mary, not David. Not after the training he's had." The doctor's voice was grim. "You've got to believe that, Mary. This is the test, the final test. He can't let us down, not now."

He could feel danger all about him. It was nothing tangible, just a deep, hollow voice in his mind, screaming out the danger. Cox shuddered, and glanced up at the brassy yellow sun, his forehead wet with perspiration. It was hot, steaming hot with an unrelenting heat that seemed to melt him down inside like soft wax. Every muscle in his body was tense; he stood poised, his pale eyes searching the barren yellow dunes of sand for the danger he knew was there.

Then the Joshua tree moved.

With a gasp, he threw himself on the sand, ten feet from it, watching it, wide-eyed. Just a slight movement of its twisted arms—he could have been mistaken, his mind could have played tricks. He trembled as he squinted through the shimmering heat at the gaunt, twisted tree.

And then, quite suddenly, realization struck him. Desert! He had been in a *tunnel*—yes, that was right, a tunnel, and that light, that roaring thing—*what was he doing here?* He sat up slowly in the sand, ran his fingers through the hot grains, studying them with infinite curiosity. No doubt about it—it *was* a desert! But how? How had he reached the tunnel in the first place? And what in the rational universe could have transported him to *this* place?

Eagerly his mind searched, striking against the curious, shadowy shield that seemed to block off his memory. There was an answer, he knew; something was wrong, he shouldn't be there. Deep in his mind he knew he was in terrible danger, but such *idiotic* danger—if he could only think, somehow remember—

His shoulders tensed, and he froze, reactively, his eyes on the yellow mound of sand across the ridge from him. Hardly breathing, he watched that yellow hillock. Then it moved again, swiftly, and froze again ten feet closer.

It had looked, in that fraction of a second, remarkably like a *cat*. A huge, savage, yellow cat. And then it had frozen into a hillock of sand.

Swiftly Cox moved, on hands and knees, at angles across

the slope away from the thing. The sand burned his hands, and he almost cried out as the grit swirled up into his eyes, but he watched, every muscle tense. It moved again, at a tangent, swiftly sliding down the slope parallel to his movement, a huge, yellow, fanged thing, moving with the grace and flowing speed of molten gold, little red eyes fixed on him. Then it froze again, melting into the yellow, shimmering sand.

Stalking him!

In blind panic he pulled himself to his feet and ran down the sandy slope away from it, his eyes burning, until a dune lay between him and the creature. Then he threw himself flat on the sand, peering over the rim of the dune. There was a flicker of yellow movement, and the sand-cat was on the slope behind him, twenty yards closer, crouching against the sand, panting hungrily.

Frantically, Cox glanced around him. No weapon! Nothing but yellow, undulating sand hills, the scorching sun and the tall, twisted Joshua trees! He looked back suddenly, and saw the sand-cat creeping toward him, slowly, slowly, not thirty yards away.

His breath came in panting gasps as he watched the creature. It was eight feet long, with lean, muscular haunches that quivered in the sun, the red eyes gleaming in savage hate. It moved with a sure confidence, a relentless certainty of its kill. Cox tried to think, tried to clear his mind of the fear and panic that gnawed at him, tried to clear away the screaming, incredulous puzzlement that tormented him. He had to get away, but he couldn't run. The creature was too fast. He knew his presence there was incredible; something in his mind tried to tell him not to believe it, that it wasn't true—but he felt the gritty sand under his sweating palms, and it was very, very real. And the sand-cat moved closer—

In a burst of speed he ran zigzagging down the slope and up the next, watching over his shoulder the flash of yellow movement. With each change in direction, the sand-cat also shifted, stalking faithfully. If only he could get out of its sight for a moment! If it wasn't too bright, if that savage brain were starved enough, he might force it into a pattern response.

He ran ten feet to the right, paused, and burst on ten feet to the left, heading toward the huge boulder which stood up like a naked sentinel on the dune ahead. The sand-cat followed, moving to the right, then to the left. Again Cox sped, sure now that the pattern would be followed, moving right, then left. A long run away from the rock, then a long run toward it. The cat was closer, just twenty yards away, closing the distance between them with each run. Panting, Cox tried to catch his breath, taking a steel grip on his nerves. He knew that panic could kill him now. Swiftly, he scuttled up over the edge of the dune, far to the right of the boulder, then abruptly switched back, keeping the boulder between him and the cat, reaching it, peering cautiously around.

It worked. Slowly, ever so slowly, the sand-cat was edging up over the dune, peering down in the direction he had run, slipping up over the dune on its belly, freezing, peering, a savage, baffled snarl coming from its dripping mouth. Eagerly Cox searched the sand around the boulder, picked up a chunk of sandstone as big as a brick. Then he took a huge breath, and plunged from behind the boulder, toward the cat, moving silently in the soft sand. With savage fury and fear he fell on the beast, raising the stone, bringing it down with all his might on the flat yellow head. The sand-cat snarled and whirled, claws slashing the air. Cox raised the stone again and again, bringing it down on the creature's skull. Razor claws ripped at his side, until the cat screamed and convulsed, and lay twitching. . . .

Suddenly there was darkness, and a cold winter breeze in his face, and the stars were twinkling in the frigid night air above him. The sand-cat was gone, the desert and the Joshua trees also. He was lying in a ditch, half-soaked in icy mud, and his side was bleeding angrily.

He stared around him, shivering. He was lying in an icy rivulet of water. Above him in the failing light he could see an embankment, topped by a low iron fence. A road! Painfully he dragged himself up toward the top and peered over.

The strip of polished metal gleamed in the starlight as icy gusts of wind and snow swept down to bite his ears and bring tears to his eyes. The tears froze on his eyelids, and the sharp coldness of the dark air bit into his lungs, bringing pain with every breath.

In the distance he heard a rumbling sound: the road trembled as the gargantuan vehicles approached. Instinctively Cox ducked below the road surface as the long line of grotesque metallic monsters roared by, glimmering within their dull fluorescent force-shields. They showed no sign of life, but rumbled past him, moving steadily down the metal highway. He could see the gaunt turrets and the gun-like projections stark against the bleak night sky. Weapons, he thought, huge, tank-like engines which lumbered and roared along the road on some errand of death.

The last of the convoy lumbered past, and David Cox eased himself cautiously up onto the road again. A burst of thunder roared in his ears. Abruptly, the rain began, huge icy drops that splattered him with the force of machine-gun bullets, stinging his skin and soaking his hair and clothes.

He shuddered, miserably, his mind groping in confusion. If

only he could find a place to *think*, somewhere to rest and collect himself, somewhere to try to dress the wound in his side. In the gloom across the road he thought he could make out the gaunt ruins of a building standing against the starlight: painfully he dragged himself across the steel strip and down into the ditch on the other side. His feet were growing numb, and the pain in his side had turned to a dull, angry throbbing, but he somehow stumbled and staggered across the field, every ounce of his strength focused on reaching some sort of shelter.

It was a building—or it had been, once. Two walls had been completely shattered, bombed out, and the roof had fallen in, but one intact wall was standing yet. Inside, the building had been gutted by fire. Cox ripped rubble and debris away from the door, forced it open on squeaking hinges. Inside he found a dry corner and located a bit of blanket from the rubble inside. He sank into the corner, shaking his head, trying desperately to orient himself.

His side had stopped bleeding. A quick examination revealed four shallow, ugly-looking lacerations running down to his thigh. Like claw marks! Of course, the sand-cat had clawed him in its last desperate snarl of rage. Cox leaned back, scratching his black hair with a grimy finger. The sand-cat had been in the *desert,* not *here*. But before that, there was a tunnel, with a roaring train bearing down on him, a train that moved without tracks. And now, a frigid, war-ravaged world—

It didn't add up. Desperately he tried to remember what had happened in between. Nothing, it seemed. He had slipped from one setting to the other in the blinking of an eye. But that was impossible! You just couldn't shift like that, from one place to another. At least, he didn't *think* it was possible.

And yet he was *here,* there was no question of that. This

building was real, the icy coldness and the darkness were very real. But the claw marks were real, too. That hadn't happened here, that had happened somewhere else. How had he come here? Had he *wanted* to come here? He shook his head angrily. It was ridiculous. But three different places—there *had* to be something in common, some common denominator. What had he found in all three places that was the same, what possible connection was there?

He saw the connection, then, and sat bolt upright, staring into the blackness. Of course, it was obvious! A tunnel, and danger. A desert, and danger. Now this cold, hostile place, *and danger!* Not danger to anyone else, just danger to himself: raw, naked danger.

He pondered this for a while. Somehow, it seemed that danger had been his entire life, that all he could think of, the only thing he had ever known, was danger. Could that be true? Instinctively, he knew it wasn't. There *had* been peace, before, somewhere, and love, and happy hours. But superimposed in his mind was the acute, barren awareness of imminent death, a sure knowledge that he could die here, abruptly, at any moment, and only his own resourcefulness could save him.

It was like repeating the well-rehearsed words of a play. Somebody had told him that. It wasn't original in his own mind. It was propaganda, conditional information, something he had been taught!

Could Mary have told him?

He gasped. Mary! He repeated the name over and over, excitedly. There was the link—Mary, his wife. Certainly there had been peace, and warmth, and comfort, and love. Mary was his wife, he had known those things with her, in some remote corner of his memory. He felt himself glow as he remembered Mary. Somewhere there had been Mary, who loved him beyond anything in the world.

The wind stirred through the ruined building, sifting damp snow down into his face. There was no Mary here. Somehow, he was here, and he was in danger, and there was no warmth nor love here. His mind swept back to reality with a jolt. He hadn't wanted to come here. It *couldn't* have been his will. There was only one other possible answer. *He had been put here.*

His mind struck the idea, and he trembled. Like the fit of a hand in a glove, the thought settled down in his mind, filling a tremendous gap. Yes, that was it, he had been placed here, for some reason. He wasn't willfully changing from place to place, he was *being changed* from place to place, against his will and volition. From danger into danger, he was being shifted, like a chessman in some horrible game of death. But no one was touching him, no one was near him—how could these changes be happening? The answer sent a chill through him, and his hand shook as he pulled his jacket tighter.

It was obvious. The changes were happening in his own mind.

He rubbed his stubbled chin. If this were true, then these things weren't really happening. He hadn't actually been in the tunnel. There hadn't actually been a sand-cat. He wasn't really lying here in a cold, damp corner, with deadly frost creeping up his legs. Angrily, he rejected the thought. There was no room for doubt, these things were real, all right. The slashes on his side were real. He knew, beyond the shadow of a doubt, that there *had* been a sand-cat. He knew it would have killed him if it could have, and if it had, he would have been quite dead.

You can die, and only your own resourcefulness will save

you. Who had said that? There had been a program, training him, somewhere, for something, something vastly important. His mind groped through the darkness, trying to penetrate the fuzzy uncertainty of his memory. Those words—from a small, red-faced man, and a tall, gaunt man in white—*Schiml!* Schiml had said those words, Schiml had put him here!

Suddenly he thought he saw the whole thing clearly. He was in danger, he must overcome the danger, he wasn't supposed to know that it wasn't really happening! There had been a long training program, with Connover, and Schiml, and all the rest, and now he was on his own. But nothing, *nothing* could really hurt him, because these things were only figments of his imagination.

He shivered in the coldness. Somehow, he didn't quite dare to believe that.

Dr. Schiml sat down on the chair and wiped drops of perspiration from his brow. His eyes were bright with excitement as he glanced at the pallid form on the bed, and then back at the red-faced Connover. "He's taken the first step," he said hoarsely. "I was sure he would."

Connover scowled and nodded, his eyes fixed on the panel beside the bed. "Yes, he took the first step all right. He's figured out the source of his environment. That's not very much."

Schiml's eyes gleamed. "When we first computed the test, you wouldn't even concede the possibility of that. Now you see that he's made it. He'll make the other steps, too."

Connover whirled angrily on the doctor. "How can he? He just *doesn't have the data!* Any fool could deduct that these are subjective mental phenomena he's facing, under the circumstances. But you're asking for the impossible if you expect him to go any further along that line of reasoning. He just doesn't have enough memory of reality to work with."

"He has Mary, and you, and me," the doctor snapped. "He knows there's been a training program, and he knows that he's being tested. And now he knows that he's living in the nightmares of his own mind. He's got to solve the rest."

"And that knowledge itself increases his danger a thousand times. He'll be reckless, overconfident—"

The girl stirred. She had been staring blankly at the man on the bed; now she looked across, at Dr. Schiml. "Connover's right," she said dully. "David has no way of knowing. He may just stand there and let himself—" she broke off helplessly.

"Mary, can't you see? That's exactly what we've got to know. We've got to know if the training was valid. He may get reckless, true, but never *too* reckless. The cat, remember? It hurt him. It *really* hurt him. He'll take the next step, all right. He may be hurt first, but he'll take it."

The girl's face flushed angrily. "It may kill him! You're asking too much, he's not a superman, he's just an ordinary, helpless man. He doesn't have any magical powers."

The doctor's face was pale. "That's right. But he does have some very un-magical powers, powers we've been drumming into his mind for the past year. He'll just have to use them, that's all. He'll *have* to."

Mary's eyes shifted once again to the motionless form on the bed. "How much proof do you need?" she asked softly. "How much more will he have to take before you stop it and bring him back?"

The doctor glanced at Connover. "Don't worry," he said gently. "I'll stop it soon enough. Just as soon as he's taken the necessary steps. But not until then."

"And if he can't make them?"

She didn't see his hand tremble as he adjusted the panel light gently. "Don't worry," he said again. "He can make them."

Gradually the numbness crept up David Cox's legs. He lay on the cold, grimy floor of the ruined building, staring into the blackness about him. His realization had brought him great relief; he was breathing more easily now, and he felt his mind relaxing from the strain he had been suffering. He knew, without question, that he was not in the midst of reality—that this cold, hostile place was *not* real, that it was merely some horrid nightmare dredged from the hidden depths of his own mind, thrust at him for some reason that he could not ponder, but thrust at him as an idiotic, horrible substitute for reality. Deep in his mind something whispered that no harm could really come. The sense of danger which pervaded his mind was false, a figment of the not-real world around him. They were testing him, it was quite obvious, though he couldn't pierce the murky shield of memory to understand *why* they were testing him.

Still, having realized the unreality, the test must be finished. He couldn't be fooled any more. He smiled to himself. Armed with that knowledge, there was no longer any danger. No real danger. Even the wound in his side was imagined, not really there at all.

Yet the cold still crept up his legs, insidiously, numbing them, moving higher and higher in his body. He didn't move. He simply waited. After all, with the test all over they would surely bring him back to reality very soon now.

Like an icy blade, something slashed at his mind, swiftly, without warning. He screamed out, writhing in agony at the savage blow. He tried to sit upright, and found his muscles numb, paralyzed. Again the blow came, sharper, more in focus, striking with vicious power that seemed to split his brain. He screamed again, closing his eyes tight, twisting on the floor. He tensed, steeling himself for another blow, and when it came his whole body jerked as he felt his own mental strength trying to rally like a protective barrier.

Frantically, he twisted and wriggled the upper part of his body, desperately and unthinkingly trying to stand and run, and toppled over onto his face in the rubble. Again the blow came, grating and screaming into his mind with an unrelenting savagery that baffled and appalled him. Crawling across the floor, he gained the door, peered sickly out into the blackness.

He could barely make out the gray shape of one of the steel monsters he had seen rumbling down the road a little before. It was resting on the rocky, frozen tundra of the field, standing motionless, the glow of power surrounding it like a ghostly aurora. He knew that the attack came from there, frightening, paralyzing bolts that shook him and sent his mind reeling helplessly, an attack of undreamed-of ferocity. He struggled, trying to erect some sort of mental patchwork against the onslaught. He had been wrong, he *could* be harmed, the test wasn't over—but why this horrible, jolting torture? Again and again the jolts came, until he screamed and writhed, and waited in agonizing anticipation of the next, and the next.

Suddenly he felt his mind sucked down into a pool of velvet soft warmth, of gentle sweetness, a welter of delightful tenderness. A wave of relief swept over him as he relaxed to the throbbing, peaceful music that whirled through his mind, sinking easily into the trap—and then, abruptly, another savage blow, out of nowhere, threw him into a curled, agonized heap on the floor. *No, no, no,* his mind screamed, *don't give up, fight it,* and he fought to reinforce a barrier, tried feebly to protect himself. This isn't real, he thought to himself, this isn't really happening, this is a ridiculous, impossible nightmare, and it *couldn't possibly hurt him*—but it *was* hurting him, until he couldn't stand it. Another blow came, wrenching his mind beyond endurance.

He knew then that death was just a few blows away. Whatever was out there in the field was trying to kill him, trying to smash him into a blubbering mass of protoplasm without mind, without life—*like the men who had come back on the star ship. . . .*

He took a gasping breath. Miraculously, he felt another link in the chain fall into place. *The star ship!* He had seen it, once, long ago. Somewhere back in a remote corner of his mind he could remember the gaunt, beaten hulk of the ship which had returned after so many years to its home on Earth, bringing home the lifeless, trampled men who had started it on its voyage. He remembered those men—barely alive, with records of unimaginable horror on their instruments, and incoherent babbling coming from their lips. Men who had gone to the stars, and met alien savagery with which they could not cope; men who had been jolted from lethargy into screaming madness at the thought of ever, ever going back to the stars again.

Was *this* why he was being tested? Was this why he had been trained, subjected to this mind-wrenching ordeal? Another blow struck him, undermining the feeble strength he had left, benumbing him, driving the picture from his mind. Was *this* what those men had faced? Was it this that had destroyed them, so infinitely far from their home, so very much alone on some alien world?

Or was it something else, something a hundred-fold more horrible? He reeled and screamed, as anger beat through to his consciousness, a certain awareness that, imagination or not, this danger was *real,* so horribly real that he was dying under the onslaught, reaching that limit of his endurance beyond which was certain death. Coldly, he searched for a weapon, coldly struggled to erect a shield to block the horrible blows, to fight horror with horror, to die fighting if need be.

Bitterly, he closed off his mind to hate and fear, dipped into the depths of horror and hatred in his mind, something to match and conquer the monstrosity he was facing. With a howl of rage he sent out searing pictures of everything he knew of savagery, of violence, of hatred and destruction, matching the alien onslaught blow for blow. They were trying to kill him, he knew they *could* kill him, and he fought them with all the strength he had, feeling the clash between his mind and the monster out in the field. They stood locked in death, swaying back and forth, up and down in utter silence, until somewhere he felt something lurch and give way. There was a scream from the field beyond, fading into silence—a scream of alien fear and hatred and defeat.

David Cox sank to the floor in exhaustion, his lips moving feebly as he groaned, "I've got to fight them, or they'll kill me—they'll kill me—they'll kill me—"

The girl was sobbing in the silent room. "Oh stop it," she groaned. "Paul, stop it! He can't go on. Oh, it's horrible."

"I've had about as much as I want to watch," Connover rasped hoarsely. His face had gone very pale, and he looked ill. "How can you go on with this?"

"It's not me that's going on with it." Dr. Schiml's voice was quiet. "I'm not concocting these things. All I'm doing is applying tiny stimuli to tiny blocks of neural tissue. Nothing more. The rest comes from his own mind."

Mary turned to him, fiercely. "How could that be true? How could there be such—such horror in his mind? *That* isn't David, you know that. David's kind, and fine, and gentle. How could he find such nightmares in his mind?"

"Everyone has nightmares in his mind, Mary. Even you. And everyone has the power of death in his mind."

"But he's taken all the steps we planned," Connover cried. "What more do you expect?"

"He's taken some of the steps," Schiml corrected angrily. "Connover, do you want to throw all these months of work out the window? Of course he's come a long way. He's realized that he's in danger that *can* kill him—that was desperately important—and he realizes the reason that he's being tested, too, though he hasn't actually rationalized it out in that way. He's beginning to realize why the star ships failed. And he's realizing that he really *must* fight for survival. From the evidence he started with, he's come a long way, a remarkably long way. Without the training, he wouldn't even have survived the tunnel. But we can't stop now. He hasn't even approached the most vital realization of all. He's too strong, too confident, not desperate enough. I can't help him, Connover. He's got to do it himself."

"But he can't survive another attack like the last," Connover snapped. "Training or no training, no man could. You're deliberately letting him kill himself, Paul. Nobody could survive more of that."

"He'll have to. The crews of the star ships couldn't. That's why they came back—the way they did."

Connover's face was working. "Well, I wash my hands off it. I'm telling you to stop now." He glared at the tall doctor. "If this boy dies, I won't be responsible."

"But you agreed—"

"Well, I've stopped agreeing. It's going too far."

Schiml stared at him for a long moment in disgust. Then he sighed. "If that's the way it's going to be, then I'll take full responsibility. But I'm going to finish."

"And if he dies?"

Schiml's eyes were dull. "It's very simple," he said. "If he dies, we'll never have another chance. There'll never be another star ship."

He couldn't tell how long he had been unconscious. Groggily, he raised his head, wincing as the pain stabbed through his skull, and blinked at the reflection of himself in the cold, mirror-steel wall. He stared at the reflection, startled to recognize himself. David Cox, his black hair muddy and caked, his face scratched in livid, grimy welts, his eyes red with strain and fatigue. With a groan, he rolled over on the polished floor, staring. Hesitantly he rubbed his side. The pain was still there, sharp under his probing fingers, and his head ached violently. But the room—

He knew that there had been another change. The room was perfectly enclosed, without a break, or window, or seam. It was a small, low-ceilinged room, with six sides—each side a polished mirror. The ceiling and floor also reflected his image as he struggled to his feet and sniffed the faint, sharp ozone smell of the room. In the mirrors, a hundred David Coxes struggled unsteadily to their feet, blinking stupidly at him and at each other. A hundred haggard, grimy David Coxes, from every angle, from behind and above, reflecting and re-reflecting in the brilliant glow of the room.

Then he heard the scream. A long, piercing, agonized scream that reverberated from the walls of the room, nearly splitting his eardrums. It came again, louder, more piercing.

Cox involuntarily clapped his fingers to his ears, but the sound came through them, pounding his skull. He heard the grinding sound along with the scream, a heavy, pervading grate of heavy-moving machinery, grinding, clanking, squealing in his ears. The scream came again, louder, more urgent, and a maddening whir joined the grating machinery. Cox stood poised in the center of the room, waiting, wary, ready for any sort of attack, his whole body geared to meet anything that came to threaten him.

Deep in his mind a weariness was growing, a smouldering anger at himself for being a party to this constantly-altering torture, at Dr. Schiml, and Connover, and anyone else who had a hand in this. What did they want? What conceivable point could there be to these attacks, this horrible instability? Why should he be subjected to such dangers that could kill him so easily? He felt a weakness, a terrible feeling that he couldn't go on, that he would have to lie down on the floor and be killed, that his limit was approaching, as he stood poised, fists clenched, waiting. How much could a man stand? What were they getting at, what did they want of him? And beyond all else, *when were they going to stop it?*

The thought broke off abruptly as a creeping chill slid up his spine, and he stared at the mirror opposite his face, almost gagging. He blinked at the image, then pawed at himself, unbelieving. Something was happening to him. Somehow, he wasn't the same any more—

Another scream cut through the air, a harsh, horrible whine of pain and torment, sending chills up his back as he winced. The image of him was different, somehow, melting and twisting before his eyes as he watched. Fascinated, he saw his hand melting away, twisting and turning into a tentacled, slimy mess of writhing worms. He tore his eyes from the image, and glanced down at the hand—and a scream tore from his own throat. His cry echoed and re-echoed, as if every mirror image was screaming too, mocking him. The room rumbled about him, with the cracking, grating sounds of machinery with sand in its gears, and the screams pierced out again and again. Now the arm was changing, too, twisting like something independently alive—

He had to get out of that room! With a scream of helpless rage he threw himself against the mirror, heard it give a strained twang as he bounced back in a heap on the floor. His mind raced, seeking a way out; he peered about, searching for a door, but there was nothing but mirrors, mirrors doing hideous things to his hand and arm, creeping upward toward his shoulder. Every time he looked for a door in one wall, he could see nothing but the reflection of another wall, and another. Down on his hands and knees, he crept about the room—four, five, six walls—was it seven and eight? Or was he repeating? He couldn't tell. Every glance drew his eyes back to the horrible, changing arm, until with superhuman control he reached down, seized the writing thing with his good hand, and wrenched it away, a twisting, quivering, jelly-like mass. The stump continued to melt and change, and he couldn't see anything but the mirror—

The thought slid through his mind, and he caught it, frantically, a straw in the wind. Reflection. He couldn't see anything but the reflection. How many walls? He couldn't count. He couldn't be sure. But he had to get out of that room, he *had* to get out! He closed his eyes, shutting out some of the brilliant light, bringing the piercing screams still closer to his mind. Slowly, painfully, he backed up to the wall of the room, keeping his eyes tightly closed, refusing to follow his actions in the mirrors, groping behind him with his good arm, seeking over the smooth surface—

A crack. Follow it. Smoothness—then metal. A knob! With a cry that was half a sob of relief he twisted the knob, felt the wall give, slipped outside onto rough, uneven ground with his eyes still closed, and slammed the door behind him. He stood panting, as the grinding and the screams peeled away like a cloak, leaving him in absolute, almost palpable silence.

There was light. He opened his eyes, then closed them again with a swift gasp, his mind rocking with shock and fear. Cautiously he opened them a slit, peering down, fighting back the terrible, age-old fear, and then slammed them shut again in a rush of vertigo.

He was standing on the top of a thousand-foot pinnacle!

Instantly he fell down flat, gripping the smooth edges of rock with a desperate grip. The section of flat rock on which he stood was the size of a coffin, six feet long and three wide. Above him was a cool, blue sky with fleecy white clouds. But on all sides, inches from where he stood, was a sheer, cruel, breath-taking drop to the pounding sea below.

A shadow passed over him, and he glanced up, tense, fearful. High above he saw huge black wings, a long, naked red neck, cruel talons, black and shiny, and a hooked beak that glinted in the sunlight. A bird like he had never seen before, sweeping down toward him, then away, making huge circles in the bright blue sky. A bird far larger than he, with evil little button-eyes that stared down at him, unblinking. . . . He sobbed, clinging lower and lower. Why? Why didn't they stop this torture? Why didn't they stop it, bring him back? He sensed that the end was near, his strength was failing, his will was failing. Little streamers of hopelessness and despair were nibbling at his brain, despair of holding out much longer, despair that was almost overpowering the fear of death which had sustained him so long.

The bird was so low he could hear the hungry flap of its wings as the steel-tipped talons swept nearer and nearer to his shoulders. He peered over the edge of the precipice, seeking some kind of descent, some toe hold, finding none. He *had* to get down, he could never fight the creature. He blinked at the blue water so far below. To climb down would be imbecility. He could feel the shredded end of his arm, loose in the cloth of his sleeve. With only one arm to hold on with, he couldn't hope to fight off the bird, even if there were a way to climb down.

A steely talon ripped his shirt as the bird skimmed by, sending a stab of pain through him, crystallizing his mad idea into action. Such a sheer drop above the water *could* mean a sheer drop below its level. An impossible choice, but there was nothing else to do. Taking a gasp of air he edged to the rim of the drop, gathered his strength, and threw himself off into space.

He struck the water with a horrible impact. It drove the wind from him, but he fought desperately toward the surface with his good arm, waiting for release, his mind begging that they would now be satisfied, that now they would stop, bring him back, not make him take any more. Finally he broke surface, and then, quite abruptly, felt solid ground under his feet. Glancing back, he saw that the pinnacle was gone, and the sky had turned a horrid orange-yellow color. Panting, his strength spent, he staggered up on the shore.

But the shore wasn't right. With a burst of anger he saw the fearful, distorted shore line upon which he stood, the sand under his feet writhing and alive as little whisps of it rose about his ankles, twisting them, as if to throw him down to his knees. Stars were blinking up at him from the ground, and great boulders of black granite scudded through the sky, whizzing past his ears like huge, unearthly cannon balls. The world was changing, turning and twisting into impossible shapes and contortions, and he smelled the dank, sharp odor of chlorine in the pungent air.

With a scream of rage he threw himself onto the writhing sand, pounding his fist against it in helpless fury, screaming out again and again. He couldn't stand it any longer, this was the end, he couldn't fight any more—they'd *have* to bring him back now, they'd *have* to stop.

A horrible thought split into his mind, bringing him to his knees abruptly. His eyes were wide, hollow-rimmed as he stared unseeing at the impossibly distorted landscape. Fear struck into him, deep, hollow fear that screamed out in his mind, a desolate, empty fear. Carefully he reviewed his ordeal, everything he had thought, and seen, and felt. For so long, he had been running, fighting—enough to satisfy any test—as much as he was humanly capable of fighting. To test his reactions, conscious and unconscious, his resourcefulness in the face of danger, his ingenuity, his resiliency, his fight, his drive, his spirit—they couldn't ask for more. Yet they still hadn't brought him back. Surely, if any human being had ever proved himself capable of surviving the fearful alienness of the stars and the worlds around the stars, he had proved himself.

But they hadn't brought him back!

The thought came again, strongly, growing into horrible certainty. He shuddered, a huge sob breaking from his lips. He knew, he was sure. He had been waiting, hoping, fighting until he had satisfied them and they would stop. But now he saw the picture, from a different angle, with terrible clarity.

They weren't going to stop. They were *never* going to stop subjecting him to these horrors. No matter how much he took, no matter how long he kept going, they would never stop.

He had been fighting for a lost cause, fighting to satisfy the insatiable. And he could keep fighting, and running, and fighting, *until he toppled over dead.*

Anger broke through the despair, blinding anger, anger that tore at his heart and twisted his mouth into a snarl of rage. He had been bilked, fooled, sold down the river. He was just another experiment, a test case, to see how much a live-danger-trained spaceman could stand, to be run to death on a treadmill like a helpless, mindless guinea pig.

For the greater good of humanity, they had said. He spat on the sand. He didn't care about humanity any more. To enable man to go to the stars! *Bother the stars!* He was a man, he'd fought a grueling battle, he'd faced death in the most horrible forms his own mind could conceive. He wasn't going to die, not in the face of the worst that Connover and Schiml and their psych-training crews could throw at him!

He leaned back on the sand, red anger tearing through his veins. It was his own mind he was fighting, these things had come from his own mind, directed by Schiml's probing needles, stimulated by tiny electrical charges, horribly real, but coming from his own mind nevertheless. They could kill him, oh yes, he never lost sight of that fact.

But he could kill *them,* too.

He saw the huge rock coming at quite a distance. It was black, and jagged, like a monstrous chunk of coal, speeding straight for his head, careening through the air like some idiotic missile from hell. With bitter anger David Cox stood up, facing the approaching boulder, fixing his mind in a single, tight channel, and screamed *"Stop!"* with all the strength he had left.

The boulder faltered in mid-flight, slowed, and vanished in a puff of blue light.

Cox turned to face the shifting, jungle-like shore line, his muscles frozen, great veins standing out in his neck. It's not true, his mind screamed to him, you can wake yourself up, they won't help you, but you can do it yourself, you can make it all go away, *you yourself can control this mind of yours.*

And then, like the mists of a dream, the world began fading away around him, twisting like wraiths in the thin, pungent air, changing, turning, changing again, as the last of his strength crept out of his beaten body, and his mind sank with the swirling world into a haze of unconsciousness. The last thing he saw before blackout was a girl's sweet face, fearful and loving, hovering close to this, calling his name. . . .

He was awake quite suddenly. Slowly, he stared around the bright, cheerful hospital room. His bed was by a window, and he looked out at the cool morning sun beaming down on the busy city below. Far below he could see the spreading buildings and grounds of the Hoffman Medical Center, like a green oasis in the teeming city. Far in the distance he saw the gleaming silver needle-points of the star ships that he knew were waiting for him.

He turned his face toward the tall, gaunt man in white by his bedside. "Paul," he said softly, "I came through."

"You came through." The doctor smiled happily, and sat down on the edge of the bed.

"But I had to terminate the test all by myself. You couldn't have stopped it for me."

Schiml nodded gravely. "That was the last step you had to take, the really critical step of the whole test. I couldn't have told the others about it, of course. They'd never have let me start the test if they had known. Connover wouldn't even stick with the part that he'd agreed upon. But without that last step, the test would have been worthless. Can you see that?"

Cox nodded slowly. "I had to rise above the physical reaction level, somehow. I had to force myself."

"There's no way for us to know what you'll find, out there, when you go," Schiml said slowly. "All we knew was what the others found, and what it did to them. They couldn't survive what they found. But we knew that training in reactive, fight-or-flight level of response to danger wouldn't be good enough, either. You would have to have razor sharp reactions *plus* full rational powers, even at the very end of your physical rope. We *had* to know that you had that."

He reached over to inspect Cox's bandaged head for a moment, his fingers infinitely gentle. "If the horrors you faced had been fakes, to be turned off when the going got tough, you wouldn't have been driven to that last ebb of resourcefulness that will save you—when you go to the stars. That was the last jump, the one the others didn't realize—that you had to discover, finally: that *we* weren't going to help you, that if you were to be saved, ultimately, it *had* to depend on you and you alone. You see, when you go where the other star men went, no one will be with you to help. It'll be you and you alone. But whatever alien worlds you find, you'll have a strange sort of guardian angel to help you."

"The training?"

"That's right. Training on an unconscious level, of course, but there in your mind nevertheless, a sharpening of your senses, of your analytical power, an overwhelmingly acute fight-or-flight sense to protect you, no matter what nightmares you run into."

Cox nodded. "I know. As you called it, at the beginning of

training—a sort of a brother. And this testing was the final step, to see if I *could* survive such nightmares."

"And you'll take it with you to the stars, the nightmare knowledge and experience, hidden deep in your mind, but it'll be there when you need it. You'll be the next man to go, you and your nightmare brother."

Cox stared out the window for a long moment. "Mary's all right?" he asked softly.

"She's waiting to see you."

David Cox sat up slowly, his mind clear in the remembrance of the ordeal he had been through. A hideous ordeal, so terrible, yet so necessary. So that when he came back, he would not be like the others had been. So that men could go to the stars with safety, and come back with safety.

Slowly he remembered his anger. He gripped the doctor's hand, squeezed it tightly. "Thanks, Paul," he said. "If I come back—"

"You mean, when you come back," said Dr. Schiml, grinning. "When you come back, we'll all have a beer together. That's what we'll do."

PRoblem

THE letter came down the slot too early that morning to be the regular mail run. Pete Greenwood eyed the New Philly photocancel with a dreadful premonition. The letter said:

> PETER:
> Can you come East chop-chop, urgent?
> Grdznth problem getting to be a PRoblem, need expert icebox salesman to get gators out of hair fast. Yes? Math boys hot on this, citizens not so hot. Please come.
>
> TOMMY

Pete tossed the letter down the gulper with a sigh. He had lost a bet to himself because it had come three days later than he expected, but it had come all the same, just as it always did when Tommy Heinz got himself into a hole.

Not that he didn't like Tommy. Tommy was a good PR-man, as PR-men go. He just didn't know his own depth. PRoblem in a beady Grdznth eye! What Tommy needed right now was a Bazooka Battalion, not a PR-man. Pete settled back in the Eastbound Rocketjet with a sigh of resignation.

He was just dozing off when the fat lady up the aisle let out a scream. A huge reptilian head had materialized out of nowhere and was hanging in air, peering about uncertainly. A scaly green body followed, four feet away, complete with long razor talons, heavy hind legs, and a whiplash tail with a needle at the end. For a moment the creature floated upside down, legs thrashing. Then the head and body joined, executed a horizontal pirouette, and settled gently to the floor like an eight-foot circus balloon.

Two rows down a small boy let out a muffled howl and tried to bury himself in his mother's coat collar. An indignant wail arose from the fat lady. Someone behind Pete groaned aloud and quickly retired behind a newspaper.

The creature coughed apologetically. "Terribly sorry," he said in a coarse rumble. "So difficult to control, you know. Terribly sorry. . . ." His voice trailed off as he lumbered down the aisle toward the empty seat next to Pete.

The fat lady gasped, and an angry murmur ran up and down the cabin. "Sit down," Pete said to the creature. "Relax. Cheerful reception these days, eh?"

"You don't mind?" said the creature.

"Not at all." Pete tossed his briefcase on the floor. At a distance the huge beast had looked like a nightmare combination of large alligator and small tyrannosaurus. Now, at close range Pete could see that the "scales" were actually tiny wrinkles of satiny green fur. He knew, of course, that the Grdznth were mammals—"docile, peace-loving mammals," Tommy's PR-blasts had declared emphatically—but with one of them sitting about a foot away Pete had to fight down a wave of horror and revulsion.

The creature was most incredibly ugly. Great yellow pouches hung down below flat reptilian eyes, and a double row of long curved teeth glittered sharply. In spite of himself Pete gripped the seat as the Grdznth breathed at him wetly through damp nostrils.

"Misgauged?" said Pete.

The Grdznth nodded sadly. "It's horrible of me, but I just can't help it. I *always* misgauge. Last time it was the chancel of St. John's Cathedral. I nearly stampeded morning prayer—" He paused to catch his breath. "What an effort. The energy barrier, you know. Frightfully hard to make the jump." He broke off sharply, staring out the window. "Dear me! Are we going *east*?"

"I'm afraid so, friend."

"Oh, dear. I wanted *Florida*."

"Well, you seem to have drifted through into the wrong airplane," said Pete. "Why Florida?"

The Grdznth looked at him reproachfully. "The Wives, of course. The climate is so much better, and they mustn't be disturbed, you know."

"Of course," said Pete. "In their condition. I'd forgotten."

"And I'm told that things have been somewhat unpleasant in the East just now," said the Grdznth.

Pete thought of Tommy, red-faced and frantic, beating off hordes of indignant citizens. "So I hear," he said. "How many more of you are coming through?"

"Oh, not many, not many at all. Only the Wives—half a million or so—and their spouses, of course." The creature clicked his talons nervously. "We haven't much more time, you know. Only a few more weeks, a few months at the most. If we couldn't have stopped over here, I just don't know *what* we'd have done."

"Think nothing of it," said Pete indulgently. "It's been great having you."

The passengers within earshot stiffened, glaring at Pete. The fat lady was whispering indignantly to her seat companion. Junior had half emerged from his mother's collar; he was busy sticking out his tongue at the Grdznth.

The creature shifted uneasily. "Really, I think—perhaps Florida would be better."

"Going to try it again right now? Don't rush off," said Pete.

"Oh, I don't mean to rush. It's been lovely, but—" Already the Grdznth was beginning to fade out.

"Try four miles down and a thousand miles southeast," said Pete.

The creature gave him a toothy smile, nodded once, and grew more indistinct. In another five seconds the seat was quite empty. Pete leaned back, grinning to himself as the angry rumble rose around him like a wave. He was a Public Relations man to the core—but right now he was off duty. He chuckled to himself, and the passengers avoided him like the plague all the way to New Philly.

But as he walked down the gangway to hail a cab, he wasn't smiling so much. He was wondering just how high Tommy was hanging him, this time.

The lobby of the Public Relations Bureau was swarming like an upturned anthill when Pete disembarked from the taxi. He could almost smell the desperate tension of the place. He fought his way past scurrying clerks and preoccupied poll-takers toward the executive elevators in the rear.

On the newly finished seventeenth floor, he found Tommy Heinz pacing the corridor like an expectant young father. Tommy had lost weight since Pete had last seen him. His ruddy face was paler, his hair thin and ragged as though chunks had been torn out from time to time. He saw Pete step off the elevator, and ran forward with open arms. "I thought you'd never get here!" he groaned. "When you didn't call, I was afraid you'd let me down."

"Me?" said Pete. "I'd never let down a pal."

The sarcasm didn't dent Tommy. He led Pete through the ante-room into the plush director's office, bouncing about excitedly, his words tumbling out like a waterfall. He looked as though one gentle shove might send him yodeling down Market Street in his underdrawers. "Hold it," said Pete. "Relax, I'm not going to leave for a while yet. Your girl screamed something about a senator as we came in. Did you hear her?"

Tommy gave a violent start. "Senator! Oh, dear." He flipped a desk switch. "What senator is that?"

"Senator Stokes," the girl said wearily. "He had an appointment. He's ready to have you fired."

"All I need now is a senator," Tommy said. "What does he want?"

"Guess," said the girl.

"Oh. That's what I was afraid of. Can you keep him there?"

"Don't worry about that," said the girl. "He's growing roots. They swept around him last night, and dusted him off this morning. His appointment was for *yesterday*, remember?"

"Remember! Of course I remember. Senator Stokes—something about a riot in Boston." He started to flip the switch, then added, "See if you can get Charlie down here with his giz."

He turned back to Pete with a frantic light in his eye. "Good old Pete. Just in time. Just. Eleventh-hour reprieve. Have a drink, have a cigar—do you want my job? It's yours. Just speak up."

"I fail to see," said Pete, "just why you had to drag me all the way from L.A. to have a cigar. I've got work to do."

"Selling movies, right?" said Tommy.

"Check."

"To people who don't want to buy them, right?"

"In a manner of speaking," said Pete testily.

"Exactly," said Tommy. "Considering some of the movies

you've been selling, you should be able to sell anything to anybody, any time, at any price."

"Please. Movies are getting Better by the Day."

"Yes, I know. And the Grdznth are getting worse by the hour. They're coming through in battalions—a thousand a day! The more Grdznth come through, the more they act as though they own the place. Not nasty or anything—it's that infernal politeness that people hate most, I think. Can't get them mad, can't get them into a fight, but they do anything they please, and go anywhere they please, and if the people don't like it, the Grdznth just go right ahead anyway."

Pete pulled at his lip. "Any violence?"

Tommy gave him a long look. "So far we've kept it out of the papers, but there have been some incidents. Didn't hurt the Grdznth a bit—they have personal protective force fields around them, a little point they didn't bother to tell us about. Anybody who tries anything fancy gets thrown like a bolt of lightning hit him. Rumors are getting wild—people saying they can't be killed, that they're just moving in to stay."

Pete nodded slowly. "Are they?"

"I wish I knew. I mean, for sure. The psych-docs say no. The Grdznth agreed to leave at a specified time, and something in their cultural background makes them stick strictly to their agreements. But that's just what the psych-docs think, and they've been known to be wrong."

"And the appointed time?"

Tommy spread his hands helplessly. "If we knew, you'd still be in L.A. Roughly six months and four days, plus or minus a month for the time differential. That's strictly tentative, according to the math boys. It's a parallel universe, one of several thousand already explored, according to the Grdznth scientists working with Charlie Karns. Most of the parallels are analogous, and we happen to be analogous to the Grdznth, a point we've omitted from our PR-blasts. They have an eight-planet system around a hot sun, and it's going to get lots hotter any day now."

Pete's eyes widened. "Nova?"

"Apparently. Nobody knows how they predicted it, but they did. Spotted it coming several years ago, so they've been romping through parallel after parallel trying to find one they can migrate to. They found one, sort of a desperation choice. It's cold and arid and full of impassable mountain chains. With an uphill fight they can make it support a fraction of their population."

Tommy shook his head helplessly. "They picked a very sensible system for getting a good strong Grdznth population on the new parallel as fast as possible. The males were picked for brains, education, ability and adaptability; the females were chosen largely according to how pregnant they were."

Pete grinned. "Grdznth in utero. There's something poetic about it."

"Just one hitch," said Tommy. "The girls can't gestate in that climate, at least not until they've been there long enough to get their glands adjusted. Seems we have just the right climate here for gestating Grdznth, even better than at home. So they came begging for permission to stop here, on the way through, to rest and parturate."

"So Earth becomes a glorified incubator." Pete got to his feet thoughtfully. "This is all very touching," he said, "but it just doesn't wash. If the Grdznth are so unpopular with the masses, why did we let them in here in the first place?" He looked narrowly at Tommy. "To be very blunt, what's the parking fee?"

"Plenty," said Tommy heavily. "That's the trouble, you

see. The fee is so high, Earth just can't afford to lose it. Charlie Karns'll tell you why."

Charlie Karns from Math Section was an intense skeleton of a man with a long jaw and a long white coat drooping over his shoulders like a shroud. In his arms he clutched a small black box.

"It's the parallel universe business, of course," he said to Pete, with Tommy beaming over his shoulder. "The Grdznth can cross through. They've been able to do it for a long time. According to our figuring, this must involve complete control of mass, space and dimension, all three. And time comes into one of the three—we aren't sure which."

The mathematician set the black box on the desk top and released the lid. Like a jack-in-the-box, two small white plastic spheres popped out and began chasing each other about in the air six inches above the box. Presently a third sphere rose up from the box and joined the fun.

Pete watched it with his jaw sagging until his head began to spin. "No wires?"

"*Strictly* no wires," said Charlie glumly. "No nothing." He closed the box with a click. "This is one of their children's toys, and theoretically, it can't work. Among other things, it takes null-gravity to operate."

Pete sat down, rubbing his chin. "Yes," he said. "I'm beginning to see. They're teaching you this?"

Tommy said, "They're trying to. He's been working for weeks with their top mathematicians, him and a dozen others. How many computers have you burned out, Charlie?"

"Four. There's a differential factor, and we can't spot it. They have the equations, all right. It's a matter of translating them into constants that make sense. But we haven't cracked the differential."

"And if you do, then what?"

Charlie took a deep breath. "We'll have inter-dimensional control, a practical, utilizable transmatter. We'll have null-gravity, which means the greatest advance in power utilization since fire was discovered. It might give us the opening to a concept of time travel that makes some kind of sense. And power! If there's an energy differential of any magnitude—" He shook his head sadly.

"We'll also know the time-differential," said Tommy hopefully, "and how long the Grdznth gestation period will be."

"It's a fair exchange," said Charlie. "We keep them until the girls have their babies. They teach us the ABC's of space, mass and dimension."

Pete nodded. "That is, if you can make the people put up with them for another six months or so."

Tommy sighed. "In a word—yes. So far we've gotten nowhere at a thousand miles an hour."

"I can't do it!" the cosmetician wailed, hurling himself down on a chair and burying his face in his hands. "I've failed. Failed!"

The Grdznth sitting on the stool looked regretfully from the cosmetician to the Public Relations men. "I say—I *am* sorry. . . ." His coarse voice trailed off as he peeled a long strip of cake makeup off his satiny green face.

Pete Greenwood stared at the cosmetician sobbing in the chair. "What's eating *him*?"

"Professional pride," said Tommy. "He can take twenty years off the face of any woman in Hollywood. But he's not getting to first base with Gorgeous over there. This is only one thing we've tried," he added as they moved on down the corridor. "You should see the field reports. We've tried selling the advances Earth will have, the wealth, the power. No dice. The man on the street reads our PR blasts, and then looks up to see one of the nasty things staring over his shoulder at the newspaper."

"So you can't make them beautiful," said Pete. "Can't you make them cute?"

"With those teeth? Those eyes? Ugh."

"How about the 'jolly company' approach?"

"Tried it. There's nothing jolly about them. They pop out of nowhere, anywhere. In church, in bedrooms, in rush-hour traffic through Lincoln Tunnel—look!"

Pete peered out the window at the traffic jam below. Cars were snarled up for blocks on either side of the intersection. A squad of traffic cops were converging angrily on the center of the mess, where a stream of green reptilian figures seemed to be popping out of the street and lumbering through the jammed autos like General Sherman tanks.

"Ulcers," said Tommy. "City traffic isn't enough of a mess as it is. And they don't *do* anything about it. They apologize profusely, but they keep coming through." The two started on for the office. "Things are getting to the breaking point. The people are wearing thin from sheer annoyance—to say nothing of the nightmares the kids are having, and the trouble with women fainting."

The signal light on Tommy's desk was flashing scarlet. He dropped into a chair with a sigh and flipped a switch. "Okay, what is it now?"

"Just another senator," said a furious male voice. "Mr. Heinz, my arthritis is beginning to win this fight. Are you going to see me now, or aren't you?"

"Yes, yes, come right in!" Tommy turned white. "Senator Stokes," he muttered. "I'd completely forgotten—"

The senator didn't seem to like being forgotten. He walked into the office, looked disdainfully at the PR-men, and sank to the edge of a chair, leaning on his umbrella.

"You have just lost your job," he said to Tommy, with an icy edge to his voice. "You may not have heard about it yet, but you can take my word for it. I personally will be delighted to make the necessary arrangements, but I doubt if I'll need to. There are at least a hundred senators in Washington who are ready to press for your dismissal, Mr. Heinz—and there's been some off-the-record talk about a lynching. Nothing official, of course."

"Senator—"

"Senator be hanged! We want somebody in this office who can manage to *do* something."

"Do something! You think I'm a magician? I can just make them vanish? What do you want me to do?"

The senator raised his eyebrows. "You needn't shout, Mr. Heinz. I'm not the least interested in *what* you do. My interest is focused completely on a collection of five thousand letters, telegrams, and visiphone calls I've received in the past three days alone. My constituents, Mr. Heinz, are making themselves clear. If the Grdznth do not go, I go."

"That would never do, of course," murmured Pete.

The senator gave Pete a cold, clinical look. "Who is this person?" he asked Tommy.

"An assistant on the job," Tommy said quickly. "A very excellent PR-man."

The senator sniffed audibly. "Full of ideas, no doubt."

"Brimming," said Pete. "Enough ideas to get your constituents off your neck for a while, at least."

"Indeed."

"Indeed," said Pete. "Tommy, how fast can you get a PR-blast to penetrate? How much medium do you control?"

"Plenty," Tommy gulped.

"And how fast can you sample response and analyze it?"

"We can have prelims six hours after the PR-blast. Pete, if you have an idea, tell us!"

Pete stood up, facing the senator. "Everything else has been tried, but it seems to me one important factor has been missed. One that will take your constituents by the ears." He looked at Tommy pityingly. "You've tried to make them lovable, but they aren't lovable. They aren't even passably attractive. There's one thing they *are* though, at least half of them."

Tommy's jaw sagged. "Pregnant," he said.

"Now see here," said the senator. "If you're trying to make a fool out of me to my face—"

"Sit down and shut up," said Pete. "If there's one thing the man in the street reveres, my friend, it's motherhood. We've got several hundred thousand pregnant Grdznth just waiting for all the little Grdznth to arrive, and nobody's given them a side glance." He turned to Tommy. "Get some copywriters down here. Get a Grdznth obstetrician or two. We're going to put together a PR-blast that will twang the people's heart-strings like a billion harps."

The color was back in Tommy's cheeks, and the senator was forgotten as a dozen intercom switches began snapping. "We'll need TV hookups, and plenty of newscast space," he said eagerly. "Maybe a few photographs—do you suppose maybe *baby* Grdznth are lovable?"

"They probably look like salamanders," said Pete. "But tell the people anything you want. If we're going to get across the sanctity of Grdznth motherhood, my friend, anything goes."

"It's genius," chortled Tommy. "Sheer genius."

"If it sells," the senator added, dubiously.

"It'll sell," Pete said. "The question is: for how long?"

The planning revealed the mark of genius. Nothing sudden, harsh, or crude—but slowly, in a radio comment here or a newspaper story there, the emphasis began to shift from Grdznth in general to Grdznth as mothers. A Rutgers professor found his TV discussion on "Motherhood as an Experience" suddenly shifted from 6:30 Monday evening to 10:30 Saturday night. Copy rolled by the ream from Tommy's office, refined copy, hypersensitively edited copy, finding its way into the light of day through devious channels.

Three days later a Grdznth miscarriage threatened, and was averted. It was only a page 4 item, but it was a beginning.

Determined movements to expel the Grdznth faltered, trembled with indecision. The Grdznth were ugly, they frightened little children, they *were* a trifle overbearing in their insufferable stubborn politeness—but in a civilized world you just couldn't turn expectant mothers out in the rain.

Not even expectant Grdznth mothers.

By the second week the blast was going at full tilt.

In the Public Relations Bureau building, machines worked on into the night. As questionnaires came back, spot candid films and street-corner interview tapes ran through the projectors on a twenty-four-hour schedule. Tommy Heinz grew thinner and thinner, while Pete nursed sharp post-prandial stomach pains.

"Why don't people *respond*?" Tommy asked plaintively on the morning the third week started. "Haven't they got any feelings? The blast is washing over them like a wave and there they sit!" He punched the private wire to Analysis for the fourth time that morning. He got a man with a hag-ridden look in his eye. "How soon?"

"You want yesterday's rushes?"

"What do you think I want? Any sign of a lag?"

"Not a hint. Last night's panel drew like a magnet. The D-Date tag you suggested has them by the nose."

"How about the President's talk?"

The man from Analysis grinned. "He should be campaigning."

Tommy mopped his forehead with his shirtsleeve. "Okay. Now listen: we need a special run on all response data we have for tolerence levels. Got that? How soon can we have it?"

Analysis shook his head. "We could only make a guess with the data so far."

"Fine," said Tommy. "Make a guess."

"Give us three hours," said Analysis.

"You've got thirty minutes. Get going."

Turning back to Pete, Tommy rubbed his hands eagerly. "It's starting to sell, boy. I don't know how strong or how good, but it's starting to sell! With the tolerance levels to tell us how long we can expect this program to quiet things down, we can give Charlie a deadline to crack his differential factor, or it's the ax for Charlie." He chuckled to himself, and paced the room in an overflow of nervous energy. "I can see it now. Open shafts instead of elevators. A quick hop to Honolulu for an afternoon on the beach, and back in time for supper. A hundred miles to the gallon for the Sunday driver. When people begin *seeing* what the Grdznth are giving us, they'll welcome them with open arms."

"Hmmm," said Pete.

"Well, why won't they? The people just didn't trust us, that was all. What does the man in the street know about trans-matters? Nothing. But give him one, and then try to take it away."

"Sure, sure," said Pete. "It sounds great. Just a little bit *too* great."

Tommy blinked at him. "Too great? Are you crazy?"

"Not crazy. Just getting nervous." Pete jammed his hands into his pockets. "Do you realize where *we're* standing in this thing? We're out on a limb—way out. We're fighting for time—time for Charlie and his gang to crack the puzzle, time for the Grdznth girls to gestate. But what are we hearing from Charlie?"

"Pete, Charlie can't just—"

"That's right," said Pete. "*Nothing* is what we're hearing from Charlie. We've got no transmatter, no null-G, no power, nothing except a whole lot of Grdznth and more coming through just as fast as they can. I'm beginning to wonder what the Grdznth *are* giving us."

"Well, they can't gestate forever."

"Maybe not, but I still have a burning desire to talk to Charlie. Something tells me they're going to be gestating a little too long."

They put through the call, but Charlie wasn't answering. "Sorry," the operator said. "Nobody's gotten through there for three days."

"Three days?" cried Tommy. "What's wrong? Is he dead?"

"Couldn't be. They burned out two more machines yesterday," said the operator. "Killed the switchboard for twenty minutes."

"Get him on the wire," Tommy said. "That's orders."

"Yes, sir. But first they want you in Analysis."

Analysis was a shambles. Paper and tape piled knee-deep on the floor. The machines clattered wildly, coughing out reams of paper to be gulped up by other machines. In a corner office they found the Analysis man, pale but jubilant.

"The Program," Tommy said. "How's it going?"

"You can count on the people staying happy for at least another five months." Analysis hesitated an instant. "If they see some baby Grdznth at the end of it all."

There was dead silence in the room. "Baby Grdznth," Tommy said finally.

"That's what I said. That's what the people are buying. That's what they'd better get."

Tommy swallowed hard. "And if it happens to be six months?"

Analysis drew a finger across his throat.

Tommy and Pete looked at each other, and Tommy's hands were shaking. "I think," he said, "we'd better find Charlie Karns right now."

Math Section was like a tomb. The machines were silent. In the office at the end of the room they found an unshaven Charlie gulping a cup of coffee with a very smug-looking Grdznth. The coffee pot was floating gently about six feet above the desk. So were the Grdznth and Charlie.

"Charlie!" Tommy howled. "We've been trying to get you for hours! The operator—"

"I know, I know." Charlie waved a hand disjointedly. "I told her to go away. I told the rest of the crew to go away, too."

"Then you cracked the differential?"

Charlie tipped an imaginary hat toward the Grdznth. "Spike cracked it," he said. "Spike is a sort of Grdznth genius." He tossed the coffee cup over his shoulder and it ricochetted in graceful slow motion against the far wall. "Now why don't you go away, too?"

Tommy turned purple. "We've got five months," he said hoarsely. "Do you hear me? If they aren't going to have their babies in five months, we're dead men."

Charlie chuckled. "Five months, he says. We figured the babies to come in about three months—right, Spike? Not that it'll make much difference to us." Charlie sank slowly down to the desk. He wasn't laughing any more. "We're never going to see any Grdznth babies. It's going to be a little too cold for that. The energy factor," he mumbled. "Nobody thought of that except in passing. Should have, though, long ago. Two completely independent universes, obviously two energy systems. Incompatible. We were dealing with mass, space and dimension—but the energy differential was the important one."

"What about the energy?"

"We're loaded with it. Super-charged. Packed to the breaking point and way beyond." Charlie scribbled frantically on the desk pad. "Look, it took energy for them to come through—immense quantities of energy. Every one that came through upset the balance, distorted our whole energy pattern. And they knew from the start that the differential was all on their side—a million of them unbalances four billion of us. All they needed to overload us completely was time for enough crossings."

"And we gave it to them." Pete sat down slowly, his face green. "Like a rubber ball with a dent in the side. Push in one side, the other side pops out. And we're the other side. When?"

"Any day now. Maybe any minute." Charlie spread his hands helplessly. "Oh, it won't be bad at all. Spike here was telling me. Mean temperature in only 39 below zero, lots of good clean snow, thousands of nice jagged mountain peaks.

A lovely place, really. Just a little too cold for Grdznth. They thought Earth was much nicer."

"For them," whispered Tommy.

"For them," Charlie said.

The Coffin Cure

WHEN the discovery was announced, it was Dr. Chauncey Patrick Coffin who announced it. He had, of course, arranged with uncanny skill to take most of the credit for himself. If it turned out to be greater than he had hoped, so much the better. His presentation was scheduled for the last night of the American College of Clinical Practitioners' annual meeting, and Coffin had fully intended it to be a bombshell.

It was. Its explosion exceeded even Dr. Coffin's wilder expectations, which took quite a bit of doing. In the end he had waded through more newspaper reporters than medical doctors as he left the hall that night. It was a heady evening for Chauncey Patrick Coffin, M.D.

Certain others were not so delighted with Coffin's bombshell.

"It's idiocy!" young Dr. Phillip Dawson wailed in the laboratory conference room the next morning. "Blind, screaming idiocy. You've gone out of your mind—that's all there is to it. Can't you see what you've done? Aside from selling your colleagues down the river, that is?" He clenched the reprint of Coffin's address in his hand and brandished it like a broadsword. " 'Report on a Vaccine for the Treatment and Cure of the Common Cold,' by C. P. Coffin, *et al.* That's what it says —*et al.* My idea in the first place. Jake and I both pounding our heads on the wall for eight solid months—and now you sneak it into publication a full year before we have any business publishing a word about it."

"Really, Phillip!" Dr. Chauncey Coffin ran a pudgy hand through his snowy hair. "How ungrateful! I thought for sure you'd be delighted. An excellent presentation, I must say—terse, succinct, unequivocal—" he raised his hand— "but *generously* unequivocal, you understand. You should have heard the ovation—they nearly went wild! And the look on Underwood's face! Worth waiting twenty years for."

"And the reporters," snapped Phillip. "Don't forget the reporters." He whirled on the small dark man sitting quietly in the corner. "How about that, Jake? Did you see the morning papers? This thief not only steals our work, he splashes it all over the countryside in red ink."

Dr. Jacob Miles coughed apologetically. "What Phillip is so stormed up about is the prematurity of it all," he said to Coffin. "After all, we've hardly had an acceptable period of clinical trial."

"Nonsense," said Coffin, glaring at Phillip. "Underwood and his men were ready to publish their discovery within another six weeks. Where would we be then? How much clinical testing do you want? Phillip, you had the worst cold of your life when you took the vaccine. Have you had any since?"

"No, of course not," said Phillip peevishly.

"Jacob, how about you? Any sniffles?"

"Oh, no. No colds."

"Well, what about those six hundred students from the University? Did I misread the reports on them?"

"No—98 per cent cured of active symptoms within twenty-four hours. Not a single recurrence. The results were just short of miraculous." Jake hesitated. "Of course, it's only been a month. . . ."

"Month, year, century! Look at them! Six hundred of the world's most luxuriant colds, and now not even a sniffle." The chubby doctor sank down behind the desk, his ruddy face beaming. "Come, now, gentlemen, be reasonable. Think positively! There's work to be done, a great deal of work. They'll be wanting me in Washington, I imagine. Press conference in twenty minutes. Drug houses to consult with. How dare we stand in the path of Progress? We've won the greatest medical triumph of all times—the conquering of the Common Cold. We'll go down in history!"

And he was perfectly right on one point, at least.

They did go down in history.

The public response to the vaccine was little less than monumental. Of all the ailments that have tormented mankind through history none was ever more universal, more tenacious, more uniformly miserable than the common cold. It was a respecter of no barriers, boundaries, or classes; ambassadors and chambermaids snuffled and sneezed in drippy-nosed unanimity. The powers in the Kremlin sniffed and blew and wept genuine tears on drafty days, while senatorial debates on earth-shaking issues paused reverently upon the unplugging of a nose, the clearing of a rhinorrheic throat. Other illnesses brought disability, even death in their wake; the common cold merely brought torment to the millions as it implacably resisted the most superhuman of efforts to curb it.

Until that chill, rainy November day when the tidings broke to the world in four inch banner heads:

COFFIN NAILS LID ON COMMON COLD

"No More Coughin' " States Co-Finder of Cure

SNIFFLES SNIPED: SINGLE SHOT TO SAVE SNEEZERS

In medical circles it was called the Coffin Multicentric Upper Respiratory Virus-Inhibiting Vaccine; but the papers could never stand for such high-sounding names, and called it, simply, "The Coffin Cure."

Below the banner heads, world-renowned feature writers expounded in reverent terms the story of the leviathan struggle of Dr. Chauncey Patrick Coffin (*et al.*) in solving this riddle of the ages: how, after years of failure, they ultimately succeeded in culturing the causative agent of the common cold, identifying it not as a single virus or group of viruses, but as a multicentric virus complex invading the soft mucous linings of the nose, throat and eyes, capable of altering its basic molecular structure at any time to resist efforts of the body from within, or the physician from without, to attack and dispel it; how the hypothesis was set forth by Dr. Phillip Dawson that the virus could be destroyed only by an antibody which could "freeze" the virus-complex in one form long enough for normal body defenses to dispose of the offending invader; the exhausting search for such a "crippling agent," and the final crowning success after injecting untold gallons of cold-virus material into the hides of a group of co-operative and forbearing dogs (a species which never suffered from colds, and hence endured the whole business with an air of affectionate boredom).

And finally, the testing. First, Coffin himself (who was suffering a particularly horrendous case of the affliction he sought to cure); then his assistants Phillip Dawson and Jacob Miles; then a multitude of students from the University—carefully chosen for the severity of their symptoms, the longevity of their colds, their tendency to acquire them on little or no provocation, and their utter inability to get rid of them with any known medical program.

They were a sorry spectacle, those students filing through the Coffin laboratory for three days in October: wheezing like steam shovels, snorting and sneezing and sniffling and blowing, coughing and squeaking, mute appeals glowing in their bloodshot eyes. The researchers dispensed the materials—a single shot in the right arm, a sensitivity control in the left.

With growing delight they then watched as the results came in. The sneezing stopped; the sniffling ceased. A great silence settled over the campus, in the classrooms, in the library, in classic halls. Dr. Coffin's voice returned (rather to the regret of his fellow workers) and he began bouncing about the laboratory like a small boy at a fair. Students by the dozen trooped in for checkups with noses dry and eyes bright.

In a matter of days there was no doubt left that the goal had been reached.

"But we have to be *sure,*" Phillip Dawson had cried cautiously. "This was only a pilot test. We need mass testing now, on an entire community. We should go to the West Coast and run studies there—they have a different breed of cold out there, I hear. We'll have to see how long the immunity lasts, make sure there are no unexpected side effects. . . ." And, muttering to himself, he fell to work with pad and pencil, calculating the program to be undertaken before publication.

But there were rumors. Underwood at Stanford, they said, had already completed his tests and was preparing a paper for publication in a matter of months. Surely with such dramatic results on the pilot tests *something* could be put into print. It would be tragic to lose the race for the sake of a little unnecessary caution. . . .

Peter Dawson was adamant, but he was a voice crying in the wilderness. Chauncey Patrick Coffin was boss.

Within a week even Coffin was wondering if he had bitten off just a trifle too much. They had expected that demand for the vaccine would be great—but even the grisly memory of the early days of the Salk vaccine had not prepared them for the mobs of sneezing, wheezing red-eyed people bombarding them for the first fruits.

Clear-eyed young men from the Government Bureau pushed through crowds of local townspeople, lining the streets outside the Coffin laboratory, standing in pouring rain to raise insistent placards.

Seventeen pharmaceutical houses descended like vultures with production plans, cost-estimates, colorful graphs demonstrating proposed yield and distribution programs. Coffin was flown to Washington, where conferences labored far into the night as demands pounded their doors like a tidal wave.

One laboratory promised the vaccine in ten days; another said a week. The first actually appeared in three weeks and two days, to be soaked up in the space of three hours by the thirsty sponge of cold-weary humanity. Express planes were dispatched to Europe, to Asia, to Africa with the precious cargo, a million needles pierced a million hides, and with a huge, convulsive sneeze mankind stepped forth into a new era.

There were abstainers, of course. There always are.

"It doesn't bake eddy differets how much you talk," Ellie

Dawson cried hoarsely, shaking her blonde curls. "I dod't wadt eddy cold shots."

"You're being totally unreasonable," Phillip said, glowering at his wife in annoyance. She wasn't the sweet young thing he had married, not this evening. Her eyes were puffy, her nose red and dripping. "You've had this cold for two solid months now, and there just isn't any sense to it. It's making you miserable. You can't eat, you can't breathe, you can't sleep."

"I dod't wadt eddy cold shots," she repeated stubbornly.

"But why not? Just one little needle, you'd hardly feel it."

"But I dod't like deedles!" she cried, bursting into tears. "Why dod't you leave be alode? Go take your dasty old deedles ad stick theb id people that wadt theb."

"Aw, Ellie—"

"I dod't care, *I dod't like deedles!*" she wailed, burying her face in his shirt.

He held her close, making comforting little noises. It was no use, he reflected sadly. Science just wasn't Ellie's long suit; she didn't know a cold vaccine from a case of smallpox, and no appeal to logic or common sense could surmount her irrational fear of hypodermics. "All right, nobody's going to make you do anything you don't want to," he said.

"Ad eddyway, thik of the poor tissue badufacturers," she sniffled, wiping her nose with a pink facial tissue. "All their little childred starvig to death."

"Say, you *have* got a cold," said Phillip, sniffing. "You've got on enough perfume to fell an ox." He wiped away tears and grinned at her. "Come on now, fix your face. Dinner at the Driftwood? I hear they have marvelous lamb chops."

It was a mellow evening. The lamb chops were delectable—the tastiest lamb chops he had ever eaten, he thought, even being blessed with as good a cook as Ellie for a spouse. Ellie dripped and blew continuously, but refused to go home until they had taken in a movie, and stopped by to dance a while. "I hardly ever gedt to see you eddy bore," she said. "All because of that dasty bedicide you're givig people."

It was true, of course. The work at the lab was endless. They danced, but came home early nevertheless. Phillip needed all the sleep he could get.

He awoke once during the night to a parade of sneezes from his wife, and rolled over, frowning sleepily to himself. It was ignominous, in a way—his own wife refusing the fruit of all those months of work.

And cold or no cold, she surely was using a whale of a lot of perfume.

He awoke, suddenly, began to stretch, and sat bolt upright in bed, staring wildly about the room. Pale morning sunlight drifted in the window. Downstairs he heard Ellie stirring in the kitchen.

For a moment he thought he was suffocating. He leaped out of bed, stared at the vanity table across the room. *"Somebody's spilled the whole damned bottle—"*

The heavy sick-sweet miasma hung like a cloud around him, drenching the room. With every breath it grew thicker. He searched the table top frantically, but there were no empty bottles. His head began to spin from the sickening effluvium.

He blinked in confusion, his hand trembling as he lit a cigarette. No need to panic, he thought. She probably knocked a bottle over when she was dressing. He took a deep puff, and burst into a paroxysm of coughing as acrid fumes burned down his throat to his lungs.

"Ellie!" He rushed into the hall, still coughing. The match

smell had given way to the harsh, caustic stench of burning weeds. He stared at his cigarette in horror and threw it into the sink. The smell grew worse. He threw open the hall closet, expecting smoke to come billowing out. "Ellie! Somebody's burning down the house!"

"Whadtever are you talking about?" Ellie's voice came from the stair well. "It's just the toast I burned, silly."

He rushed down the stairs two at a time—and nearly gagged as he reached the bottom. The smell of hot, rancid grease struck him like a solid wall. It was intermingled with an oily smell of boiled and parboiled coffee, overpowering in its intensity. By the time he reached the kitchen he was holding his nose, tears pouring from his eyes. *"Ellie, what are you doing in here*?"

She stared at him. "I'b baking breakfast."

"But don't you *smell* it?"

"Sbell whadt?" said Ellie.

On the stove the automatic percolator was making small, promising noises. In the frying pan four sunnyside eggs were sizzling; half a dozen strips of bacon drained on a paper towel on the sideboard. It couldn't have looked more innocent.

Cautiously, Phillip released his nose, sniffed. The stench nearly choked him. "You mean you don't smell anything *strange*?"

"I did't sbell eddythig, period," said Eddie defensively.

"The coffee, the bacon—*come here a minute*."

She reeked—of bacon, of coffee, of burned toast, but mostly of perfume. "Did you put on any fresh perfume this morning?"

"Before breakfast? Dod't be ridiculous."

"Not even a drop?" Phillip was turning very white.

"Dot a drop."

He shook his head. "Now, wait a minute. This must be all

in my mind. I'm—just imagining things, that's all. Working too hard, hysterical reaction. In a minute it'll all go away." He poured a cup of coffee, added cream and sugar.

But he couldn't get it close enough to taste it. It smelled as if it had been boiling three weeks in a rancid pot. It was the smell of coffee, all right, but a smell that was fiendishly distorted, overpoweringly, nauseatingly magnified. It pervaded the room and burned his throat and brought tears gushing to his eyes.

Slowly, realization began to dawn. He spilled the coffee as he set the cup down. The perfume. The coffee. The cigarette. . . .

"My hat," he choked. "Get me my hat. I've got to get to the laboratory."

It got worse all the way downtown. He fought down waves of nausea as the smell of damp, rotting earth rose from his front yard in a gray cloud. The neighbor's dog dashed out to greet him, exuding the great-grandfather of all doggy odors. As Phillip waited for the bus, every passing car fouled the air with noxious fumes, gagging him, doubling him up with coughing as he dabbed at his streaming eyes.

Nobody else seemed to notice anything wrong at all.

The bus ride was a nightmare. It was a damp, rainy day; the inside of the bus smelled like the men's locker room after a big game. A bleary-eyed man with three-days' stubble on his chin flopped down in the seat next to him, and Phillip reeled back with a jolt to the job he had held in his student days, cleaning vats in the brewery.

"It'sh a great morning," Bleary-eyes breathed at him, "huh, Doc?" Phillip blanched. To top it, the man had had a breakfast of salami. In the seat ahead, a fat man held a dead cigar clamped in his mouth like a rank growth. Phillip's stomach began rolling; he sank his face into his hand, trying unobtrusively to clamp his nostrils. With a groan of deliverance he lurched off the bus at the laboratory gate.

He met Jake Miles coming up the steps. Jake looked pale, too pale.

"Morning," Phillip said weakly. "Nice day. Looks like the sun might come through."

"Yeah," said Jake. "Nice day. You—uh—feel all right this morning?"

"Fine, fine." Phillip tossed his hat in the closet, opened the incubator on his culture tubes, trying to look busy. He slammed the door after one whiff and gripped the edge of the work table with whitening nuckles. "Why?"

"Oh, nothing. Thought you looked a little peaked, was all."

They stared at each other in silence. Then, as though by signal, their eyes turned to the office at the end of the lab.

"Coffin come in yet?"

Jake nodded. "He's in there. He's got the door locked."

"I think he's going to have to open it," said Phillip.

A gray-faced Dr. Coffin unlocked the door, backed quickly toward the wall. The room reeked of kitchen deodorant. "Stay right where you are," Coffin squeaked. "Don't come a step closer. I can't see you now. I'm—I'm busy, I've got work that has to be done—"

"You're telling *me*," growled Phillip. He motioned Jake into the office and locked the door carefully. Then he turned to Coffin. "When did it start for you?"

Coffin was trembling. "Right after supper last night. I thought I was going to suffocate. Got up and walked the streets all night. My God, what a stench!"

"Jake?"

Dr. Miles shook his head. "Sometime this morning, I don't know when. I woke up with it."

"That's when it hit me," said Phillip.

"But I don't understand," Coffin howled. "Nobody else seems to notice anything—"

"Yet," said Phillip, "we were the first three to take the Coffin Cure, remember? You, and me and Jake. Two months ago."

Coffin's forehead was beaded with sweat. He stared at the two men in growing horror. *"But what about the others?"* he whispered.

"I think," said Phillip, "that we'd better find something spectacular to do in a mighty big hurry. That's what I think."

Jake Miles said, "The most important thing right now is secrecy. We mustn't let a word get out, not until we're absolutely certain."

"But what's *happened?"* Coffin cried. "These foul smells, everywhere. You, Phillip, you had a cigarette this morning. I can smell it clear over here, and it's bringing tears to my eyes. And if I didn't know better I'd swear neither of you had had a bath in a week. Every odor in town has suddenly turned foul—"

"Magnified, you mean," said Jake. "Perfume still smells sweet—there's just too much of it. The same with cinnamon; I tried it. Cried for half an hour, but it still smelled like cinnamon. No, I don't think the *smells* have changed any."

"But what, then?"

"Our noses have changed, obviously." Jake paced the floor in excitement. "Look at our dogs! They've never had colds—and they practically live by their noses. Other animals—all dependent on their senses of smell for survival—and none of them ever have anything even vaguely reminiscent of a common cold. The multicentric virus hits primates only—*and it reaches its fullest parasitic powers in man alone!*"

Coffin shook his head miserably. "But why this horrible stench all of a sudden? I haven't had a cold in weeks—"

"Of course not! That's just what I'm trying to say," Jake cried. "Look, why do we have any sense of smell at all? Because we have tiny olfactory nerve endings buried in the mucous membrane of our noses and throats. But we have always had the virus living there, too, colds or no colds, throughout our entire lifetime. It's *always* been there, anchored in the same cells, parasitizing the same sensitive tissues that carry our olfactory nerve endings, numbing them and crippling them, making them practically useless as sensory organs. No wonder we never smelled anything before! Those poor little nerve endings never had a chance!"

"Until we came along in our shining armor and destroyed the virus," said Phillip.

"Oh, we didn't destroy it. We merely stripped it of a very slippery protective mechanism against normal body defences." Jake perched on the edge of the desk, his dark face intense. "These two months since we had our shots have witnessed a battle to the death between our bodies and the virus. With the help of the vaccine, our bodies have won, that's all—stripped away the last vestiges of an invader that has been almost a part of our normal physiology since the beginning of time. And now for the first time those crippled little nerve endings are just beginning to function."

"God help us," Coffin groaned. "You think it'll get worse?"

"And worse. And still worse," said Jake.

"I wonder," said Phillip slowly, "what the anthropologists will say."

"What do you mean?"

"Maybe it was just a single mutation somewhere back there. Just a tiny change of cell structure or metabolism that left one line of primates vulnerable to an invader no other would harbor. Why else should man have begun to flower and blossom intellectually—grow to depend so much on his brains instead of his brawn that he could rise above all others? What better reason than because somewhere along the line in the world of fang and claw *he suddenly lost his sense of smell?*"

They stared at each other. "Well, he's got it back again now," Coffin wailed, "and he's not going to like it a bit."

"No, he surely isn't," Jake agreed. "He's going to start looking very quickly for someone to blame, I think."

They both looked at Coffin.

"Now don't be ridiculous, boys," said Coffin, turning white. "We're in this together. Phillip, it was your idea in the first place—you said so yourself! You can't leave me now—"

The telephone jangled. They heard the frightened voice of the secretary clear across the room. "Dr. Coffin? There was a student on the line just a moment ago. He—he said he was coming up to see you. Now, he said, not later."

"I'm busy," Coffin sputtered. "I can't see anyone. And I can't take any calls."

"But he's already on his way up," the girl burst out. "He was saying something about tearing you apart with his bare hands."

Coffin slammed down the receiver. His face was the color of lead. "They'll crucify me!" he sobbed. "Jake—Phillip—you've got to help me."

Phillip sighed and unlocked the door. "Send a girl down to the freezer and have her bring up all the live cold virus she can find. Get us some inoculated monkeys and a few dozen dogs." He turned to Coffin. "And stop sniveling. You're the big publicity man around here; you're going to handle the screaming masses, whether you like it or not."

"But what are you going to do?"

"I haven't the faintest idea," said Phillip, "but whatever I do is going to cost you your shirt. We're going to find out how to catch cold again if we have to die."

It was an admirable struggle, and a futile one. They sprayed their noses and throats with enough pure culture of virulent live virus to have condemned an ordinary man to a lifetime of sneezing, watery-eyed misery. They didn't develop a sniffle among them. They mixed six different strains of virus and gargled the extract, spraying themselves and every inoculated monkey they could get their hands on with the vile-smelling stuff. Not a sneeze. They injected it hypodermically, intradermally, subcutaneously, intramuscularly, and intravenously. They drank it. They bathed in the stuff.

But they didn't catch a cold.

"Maybe it's the wrong approach," Jake said one morning. "Our body defenses are keyed up to top performance right now. Maybe if we break them down we can get somewhere."

They plunged down that alley with grim abandon. They starved themselves. They forced themselves to stay awake for days on end, until exhaustion forced their eyes closed in spite of all they could do. They carefully devised vitamin-free, protein-free, mineral-free diets that tasted like library paste and smelled worse. They wore wet clothes and sopping shoes to work, turned off the heat and threw windows open to the raw winter air. Then they resprayed themselves with the live cold virus and waited reverently for the sneezing to begin.

It didn't. They stared at each other in gathering gloom. They'd never felt better in their lives.

Except for the smells, of course. They'd hoped that they might, presently, get used to them. They didn't. Every day it grew a little worse. They began smelling smells they never dreamed existed—noxious smells, cloying smells, smells that drove them gagging to the sinks. Their nose-plugs were rapidly losing their effectiveness. Mealtimes were nightmarish ordeals; they lost weight with alarming speed.

But they didn't catch cold.

"*I* think you should all be locked up," Ellie Dawson said severely as she dragged her husband, blue-faced and shivering, out of an icy shower one bitter morning. "You've lost your wits. You need to be protected against yourselves, that's what you need."

"You don't understand," Phillip moaned. "We've *got* to catch cold."

"Why?" Ellie snapped angrily. "Suppose you don't—what's going to happen?"

"We had three hundred students march on the laboratory today," Phillip said patiently. "The smells were driving them crazy, they said. They couldn't even bear to be close to their best friends. They wanted something done about it, or else they wanted blood. Tomorrow we'll have them back and three hundred more. And they were just the pilot study! What's going to happen when fifteen million people find their noses going bad on them?" He shuddered. "Have you seen the papers? People are already going around sniffing like bloodhounds. And *now* we're finding out what a thorough job we did. We can't crack it, Ellie. We can't even get a toe hold. Those antibodies are just doing too good a job."

"Well, maybe you can find some unclebodies to take care of them," Ellie offered vaguely.

"Look, don't make bad jokes—"

"I'm not making jokes! All I want is a husband back who doesn't complain about how everything smells, and eats the dinners I cook, and doesn't stand around in cold showers at six in the morning."

"I know it's miserable," he said helplessly. "But I don't know how to stop it."

He found Jake and Coffin in tight-lipped conference when he reached the lab. "I can't do it any more," Coffin was saying. "I've begged them for time. I've threatened them. I've promised them everything but my upper plate. I can't face them again, I just can't."

"We only have a few days left," Jake said grimly. "If we don't come up with something, we're goners."

Phillip's jaw suddenly sagged as he stared at them. "You know what I think?" he said suddenly. "I think we've been prize idiots. We've gotten so rattled we haven't used our heads. And all the time it's been sitting there blinking at us!"

"What are you talking about?" snapped Jake.

"Unclebodies," said Phillip.

"Oh, great God!"

"No, I'm serious." Phillip's eyes were very bright. "How many of those students do you think you can corral to help us?"

Coffin gulped. "Six hundred. They're out there in the street right now, howling for a lynching."

"All right, I want them in here. And I want some monkeys. Monkeys with colds, the worse colds the better."

"Do you have any idea what you're doing?" asked Jake.

"None in the least," said Phillip happily, "except that it's never been done before. But maybe it's time we tried following our noses for a while."

The tidal wave began to break two days later . . . only a few people here, a dozen there, but enough to confirm the direst newspaper predictions. The boomerang was completing its circle.

At the laboratory the doors were kept barred, the telephones disconnected. Within, there was a bustle of feverish—if odorous—activity. For the three researchers, the olfactory acuity had reached agonizing proportions. Even the small gas masks Phillip had devised could no longer shield them from the constant barrage of violent odors.

But the work went on in spite of the smell. Truckloads of monkeys arrived at the lab—cold-ridden monkeys, sneezing, coughing, weeping, wheezing monkeys by the dozen. Culture trays bulged with tubes, overflowed the incubators and work tables. Each day six hundred angry students paraded through the lab, arms exposed, mouths open, grumbling but co-operating.

At the end of the first week, half the monkeys were cured of their colds and were quite unable to catch them back; the other half had new colds and couldn't get rid of them. Phillip observed this fact with grim satisfaction, and went about the laboratory mumbling to himself.

Two days later he burst forth jubilantly, lugging a sad-looking puppy under his arm. It was like no other puppy in the world. This puppy was sneezing and snuffling with a perfect howler of a cold.

The day came when they injected a tiny droplet of milky fluid beneath the skin of Phillip's arm, and then got the virus spray and gave his nose and throat a liberal application. Then they sat back and waited.

They were still waiting three days later.

"It was a great idea," Jake said gloomily, flipping a bulging notebook closed with finality. "It just didn't work, was all."

Phillip nodded. Both men had grown thin, with pouches under their eyes. Jake's right eye had begun to twitch uncontrollably whenever anyone came within three yards of him. "We can't go on like this, you know. The people are going wild."

"Where's Coffin?"

"He collapsed three days ago. Nervous prostration. He kept having dreams about hangings."

Phillip sighed. "Well, I suppose we'd better just face it. Nice knowing you, Jake. Pity it had to be this way."

"It was a great try, old man. A great try."

"Ah, yes. Nothing like going down in a blaze of—"

Phillip stopped dead, his eyes widening. His nose began to twitch. He took a gasp, a larger gasp, as a long-dead reflex came sleepily to life, shook its head, reared back . . .

Phillip sneezed.

He sneezed for ten minutes without a pause, until he lay on the floor blue-faced and gasping for air. He caught hold of Jake, wringing his hand as tears gushed from his eyes. He gave his nose an enormous blow, and headed shakily for the telephone.

"It was a sipple edough pridciple," he said later to Ellie as she spread mustard on his chest and poured more warm water into his foot bath. "The Cure itself depedded upod it —the adtiged-adtibody reactiod. We had the adtibody agaidst the virus, all ridght; what we had to find was sobe kide of adtibody agaidst the *adtibody*." He sneezed violently, and poured in nose drops with a happy grin.

"Will they be able to make it fast enough?"

"Just aboudt fast edough for people to get good ad eager to catch cold agaid," said Phillip. "There's odly wud little hitch. . . ."

Ellie Dawson took the steaks from the grill and set them, still sizzling, on the dinner table. "Hitch?"

Phillip nodded as he chewed the steak with a pretence of enthusiasm. It tasted like slightly damp K-ration.

"This stuff we've bade does a real good job. Just a little too good." He wiped his nose and reached for a fresh tissue.

"I bay be wrog, but I thik I've got this cold for keeps," he said sadly. "Udless I cad fide ad adtibody agaidst the adtibody agaidst the adtibody—"

Brightside Crossing

JAMES BARON was not pleased to hear that he had had a visitor when he reached the Red Lion that evening. He had no stomach for mysteries, vast or trifling, and there were pressing things to think about at this time. Yet the doorman had flagged him as he came in from the street: "A thousand pardons, Mr. Baron. The gentleman—he would leave no name. He said you'd want to see him. He will be back by eight."

Now Baron drummed his fingers on the table top, staring about the quiet lounge. Street trade was discouraged at the Red Lion, gently but persuasively; the patrons were few in number. Across to the right was a group that Baron knew vaguely—Andean climbers, or at least two of them were. Over near the door he recognized old Balmer, who had mapped the first passage to the core of Vulcan Crater on Venus. Baron returned his smile with a nod. Then he settled back and waited impatiently for the intruder who demanded his time without justifying it.

Presently a small, grizzled man crossed the room and sat down at Baron's table. He was short and wiry. His face held no key to his age—he might have been thirty or a thousand—but he looked weary and immensely ugly. His cheeks and forehead were twisted and brown, with scars that were still healing.

The stranger said, "I'm glad you waited. I've heard you're planning to attempt the Brightside."

Baron stared at the man for a moment. "I see you can read telecasts," he said coldly. "The news was correct. We are going to make a Brightside Crossing."

"At perihelion?"

"Of course. When else?"

The grizzled man searched Baron's face for a moment without expression. Then he said slowly, "No, I'm afraid you're not going to make the Crossing."

"Say, who are you, if you don't mind?" Baron demanded.

"The name is Claney," said the stranger.

There was a silence. Then: "Claney? *Peter* Claney?"

"That's right."

Baron's eyes were wide with excitement, all trace of anger gone. "Great balls of fire, man—*where have you been hiding?* We've been trying to contact you for months!"

"I know. I was hoping you'd quit looking and chuck the whole idea."

"Quit looking!" Baron bent forward over the table. "My friend, we'd given up hope, but we've never quit looking. Here, have a drink. There's so much you can tell us." His fingers were trembling.

Peter Claney shook his head. "I can't tell you anything you want to hear."

"But you've *got* to. You're the only man on Earth who's attempted a Brightside Crossing and lived through it! And the story you cleared for the news—it was nothing. We need *details*. Where did your equipment fall down? Where did you miscalculate? What were the trouble spots?" Baron jabbed a finger at Claney's face. "That, for instance—epithelioma? Why? What was wrong with your glass? Your filters? We've got to know those things. If you can tell us, we can make it across where your attempt failed—"

"You want to know why we failed?" asked Claney.

"Of course we want to know. We *have* to know."

"It's simple. We failed because it can't be done. We couldn't do it and neither can you. No human beings will ever cross the Brightside alive, not if they try for centuries."

"Nonsense," Baron declared. "We will."

Claney shrugged. "I was there. I know what I'm saying. You can blame the equipment or the men—there were flaws in both quarters—but we just didn't know what we were fighting. It was the *planet* that whipped us, that and the *Sun*. They'll whip you, too, if you try it."

"Never," said Baron.

"Let me tell you," Peter Claney said.

I'd been interested in the Brightside for almost as long as I can remember (Claney said). I guess I was about ten when Wyatt and Carpenter made the last attempt—that was in 2082, I think. I followed the news stories like a tri-V serial and then I was heartbroken when they just disappeared.

I know now that they were a pair of idiots, starting off without proper equipment, with practically no knowledge of surface conditions, without any charts—they couldn't have made a hundred miles—but I didn't know that then and it was a terrible tragedy. After that, I followed Sanderson's work in the Twilight Lab up there and began to get Brightside into my blood, sure as death.

But it was Mikuta's idea to attempt a Crossing. Did you ever know Tom Mikuta? I don't suppose you did. No, not Japanese—Polish-American. He was a major in the Interplanetary Service for some years and hung onto the title after he gave up his commission.

He was with Armstrong on Mars during his Service days, did a good deal of the original mapping and surveying for the Colony there. I first met him on Venus; we spent five years together up there doing some of the nastiest exploring since the Matto Grasso. Then he made the attempt on Vulcan Crater that paved the way for Balmer a few years later.

I'd always liked the Major—he was big and quiet and cool, the sort of guy who always had things figured a little further ahead than anyone else and always knew what to do in a tight place. Too many men in this game are all nerve and luck, with no judgment. The Major had both. He also had the kind of personality that could take a crew of wild men and make them work like a well-oiled machine across a thousand miles of Venus jungle. I liked him and I trusted him.

He contacted me in New York and he was very casual at first. We spent an evening here at the Red Lion, talking about old times; he told me about the Vulcan business, and how he'd been out to see Sanderson and the Twilight Lab on Mercury, and how he preferred a hot trek to a cold one any day of the year—and then he wanted to know what I'd been doing since Venus and what my plans were.

"No particular plans," I told him. "Why?"

He looked me over. "How much do you weigh, Peter?"

I told him one-thirty-five.

"That much!" he said. "Well, there can't be much fat on you, at any rate. How do you take heat?"

"You should know," I said. "Venus was no icebox."

"No, I mean *real* heat."

Then I began to get it. "You're planning a trip."

"That's right. A hot trip." He grinned at me. "Might be dangerous, too."

"What trip?"

"Brightside of Mercury," the Major said.

I whistled cautiously. "At aphelion?"

He threw his head back. "Why try a Crossing at aphelion? What have you done then? Four thousand miles of butcherous heat, just to have some joker come along, use your data and drum you out of the glory by crossing at perihelion forty-four days later? No, thanks. I want the Brightside without any nonsense about it." He leaned across me eagerly. "I want to make a Crossing at perihelion and I want to cross on the surface. If a man can do that, he's got Mercury. Until then, *nobody's* got Mercury. I want Mercury—but I'll need help getting it."

I'd thought of it a thousand times and never dared consider it. Nobody had, since Wyatt and Carpenter disappeared. Mercury turns on its axis in the same time that it wheels around the Sun, which means that the Brightside is always facing in. That makes the Brightside of Mercury at perihelion the hottest place in the Solar System, with one single exception: the surface of the Sun itself.

It would be a hellish trek. Only a few men had ever learned just *how* hellish and they never came back to tell about it. It was a real hell's Crossing, but someday, I thought, somebody would cross it.

I wanted to be along.

The twilight lab, near the northern pole of Mercury, was the obvious jumping-off place. The setup there wasn't very extensive—a rocket landing, the labs and quarters for Sanderson's crew sunk deep into the crust, and the tower that housed the Solar 'scope that Sanderson had built up there ten years before.

Twilight Lab wasn't particularly interested in the Brightside, of course—the Sun was Sanderson's baby and he'd picked Mercury as the closest chunk of rock to the Sun that could hold his observatory. He'd chosen a good location, too. On Mercury, the Brightside temperature hits 770° F. at perihelion and the Darkside runs pretty constant at −410° F. No permanent installation with a human crew could survive at either extreme. But with Mercury's wobble, the twilight zone between Brightside and Darkside offers something closer to survival temperatures.

Sanderson built the Lab up near the pole, where the zone is about five miles wide, so the temperature only varies 50 to 60 degrees with the libration. The Solar 'scope could take that much change and they'd get good clear observation of the Sun for about seventy out of the eighty-eight days it takes the planet to wheel around.

The Major was counting on Sanderson knowing something about Mercury as well as the Sun when we camped at the Lab to make final preparations.

Sanderson did. He thought we'd lost our minds and he said so, but he gave us all the help he could. He spent a week briefing Jack Stone, the third member of our party, who had arrived with the supplies and equipment a few days earlier. Poor Jack met us at the rocket landing almost bawling, Sanderson had given him such a gloomy picture of what Brightside was like.

Stone was a youngster—hardly twenty-five, I'd say—but he'd been with the Major at Vulcan and had begged to join this trek. I had a funny feeling that Jack really didn't care for exploring too much, but he thought Mikuta was God, followed him around like a puppy.

It didn't matter to me as long as he knew what he was getting in for. You don't go asking people in this game why they do it —they're liable to get awfully uneasy and none of them can ever give you an answer that makes sense. Anyway, Stone had borrowed three men from the Lab, and had the supplies and equipment all lined up when we got there, ready to check and test.

We dug right in. With plenty of funds—tri-V money and some government cash the Major had talked his way around— our equipment was new and good. Mikuta had done the designing and testing himself, with a big assist from Sanderson. We had four Bugs, three of them the light pillow-tire models, with special lead-cooled cut-in engines when the heat set in, and one heavy-duty tractor model for pulling the sledges.

The Major went over them like a kid at the circus. Then he said, "Have you heard anything from McIvers?"

"Who's he?" Stone wanted to know.

"He'll be joining us. He's a good man—got quite a name for climbing, back home." The Major turned to me. "You've probably heard of him."

I'd heard plenty of stories about Ted McIvers and I wasn't too happy to hear that he was joining us. "Kind of a daredevil, isn't he?"

"Maybe. He's lucky and skillful. Where do you draw the line? We'll need plenty of both."

"Have you ever worked with him?" I asked.

"No. Are you worried?"

"Not exactly. But Brightside is no place to count on luck."

The Major laughed. "I don't think we need to worry about McIvers. We understood each other when I talked up the trip to him and we're going to need each other too much to do any fooling around." He turned back to the supply list. "Meanwhile, let's get this stuff listed and packed. We'll need to cut weight sharply and our time is short. Sanderson says we should leave in three days."

Two days later, McIvers hadn't arrived. The Major didn't say much about it. Stone was getting edgy and so was I. We spent the second day studying charts of the Brightside, such as they were. The best available were pretty poor, taken from so far out that the detail dissolved into blurs on blow-up. They showed the biggest ranges of peaks and craters and faults, and that was all. Still, we could use them to plan a broad outline of our course.

"This range here," the Major said as we crowded around the board, "is largely inactive, according to Sanderson. But these to the south and west *could* be active. Seismograph tracings suggest a lot of activity in that region, getting worse down toward the equator—not only volcanic, but sub-surface shifting."

Stone nodded. "Sanderson told me there was probably constant surface activity."

The Major shrugged. "Well, it's treacherous, there's no doubt of it. But the only way to avoid it is to travel over the Pole, which would lose us days and offer us no guarantee of less activity to the west. Now we might avoid some if we could find a pass through this range and cut sharp east—"

It seemed that the more we considered the problem, the further we got from a solution. We knew there were active volcanoes on the Brightside—even on the Darkside, though surface activity there was pretty much slowed down and localized.

But there were problems of atmosphere on Brightside, as

well. There *was* an atmosphere and a constant atmospheric flow from Brightside to Darkside. Not much—the lighter gases had reached escape velocity and disappeared from Brightside millennia ago—but there was CO_2, and nitrogen, and traces of other heavier gases. There was also an abundance of sulfur vapor, as well as carbon disulfide and sulfur dioxide.

The atmospheric tide moved toward the Darkside, where it condensed, carrying enough volcanic ash with it for Sanderson to estimate the depth and nature of the surface upheavals on Brightside from his samplings. The trick was to find a passage that avoided those upheavals as far as possible. But in the final analysis, we were barely scraping the surface. The only way we would find out what was happening where was to be there.

Finally, on the third day, McIvers blew in on a freight rocket from Venus. He'd missed the ship that the Major and I had taken by a few hours, and had conned his way to Venus in hopes of getting a hop from there. He didn't seem too upset about it, as though this were his usual way of doing things and he couldn't see why everyone should get so excited.

He was a tall, rangy man with long, wavy hair prematurely gray, and the sort of eyes that looked like a climber's—half-closed, sleepy, almost indolent, but capable of abrupt alertness. And he never stood still; he was always moving, always doing something with his hands, or talking, or pacing about.

Evidently the Major decided not to press the issue of his arrival. There was still work to do, and an hour later we were running the final tests on the pressure suits. That evening, Stone and McIvers were thick as thieves, and everything was set for an early departure after we got some rest.

"And that," said Baron, finishing his drink and signaling the waiter for another pair, "was your first big mistake."

Peter Claney raised his eyebrows. "McIvers?"

"Of course."

Claney shrugged, glanced at the small quiet tables around them. "There are lots of bizarre personalities around a place like this, and some of the best wouldn't seem to be the most reliable at first glance. Anyway, personality problems weren't our big problem right then. *Equipment* worried us first and *route* next."

Baron nodded in agreement. "What kind of suits did you have?"

"The best insulating suits ever made," said Claney. "Each one had an inner lining of a fiberglass modification, to avoid the clumsiness of asbestos, and carried the refrigerating unit and oxygen storage which we recharged from the sledges every eight hours. Outer layer carried a monomolecular chrome reflecting surface that made us glitter like Christmas trees. And we had a half-inch dead-air space under positive pressure between the two layers. Warning thermocouples, of course—at 770 degrees, it wouldn't take much time to fry us to cinders if the suits failed somewhere."

"How about the Bugs?"

"They were insulated, too, but we weren't counting on them too much for protection."

"You weren't!" Baron exclaimed. "Why not?"

"We'd be in and out of them too much. They gave us mobility and storage, but we knew we'd have to do a lot of forward work on foot." Claney smiled bitterly. "Which meant that we had an inch of fiberglass and a half-inch of dead air between us and a surface temperature where lead flowed like water and zinc was almost at melting point and the pools of sulfur in the shadows were boiling like oatmeal over a campfire."

Baron licked his lips. His fingers stroked the cool, wet glass as he set it down on the tablecloth.

"Go on," he said tautly. "You started on schedule?"

"Oh, yes," said Claney, "we started on schedule, all right. We just didn't quite end on schedule, that was all. But I'm getting to that."

He settled back in his chair and continued.

We jumped off from Twilight on a course due southeast with thirty days to make it to the Center of Brightside. If we could cross an average of seventy miles a day, we could hit Center exactly at perihelion, the point of Mercury's closest approach to the Sun—which made Center the hottest part of the planet at the hottest it ever gets.

The Sun was already huge and yellow over the horizon when we started, twice the size it appears on Earth. Every day that Sun would grow bigger and whiter, and every day the surface would get hotter. But once we reached Center, the job was only half done—we would still have to travel another two thousand miles to the opposite twilight zone. Sanderson was to meet us on the other side in the Laboratory's scout ship, approximately sixty days from the time we jumped off.

That was the plan, in outline. It was up to us to cross those seventy miles a day, no matter how hot it became, no matter what terrain we had to cross. Detours would be dangerous and time-consuming. Delays could cost us our lives. We all knew that.

The Major briefed us on details an hour before we left. "Peter, you'll take the lead Bug, the small one we stripped down for you. Stone and I will flank you on either side, giving you a hundred-yard lead. McIvers, you'll have the job of dragging the sledges, so we'll have to direct your course pretty closely. Peter's job is to pick the passage at any given point. If there's any doubt of safe passage, we'll all explore ahead on foot before we risk the Bugs. Got that?"

McIvers and Stone exchanged glances. McIvers said: "Jack and I were planning to change around. We figured he could take the sledges. That would give me a little more mobility."

The Major looked up sharply at Stone. "Do you buy that, Jack?"

Stone shrugged. "I don't mind. Mac wanted—"

McIvers made an impatient gesture with his hands. "It doesn't matter. I just feel better when I'm on the move. Does it make any difference?"

"I guess it doesn't," said the Major. "Then you'll flank Peter along with me. Right?"

"Sure, sure." McIvers pulled at his lower lip. "Who's going to do the advance scouting?"

"It sounds like I am," I cut in. "We want to keep the lead Bug light as possible."

Mikuta nodded. "That's right. Peter's Bug is stripped down to the frame and wheels."

McIvers shook his head. "No, I mean the *advance* work. You need somebody out ahead—four or five miles, at least—to pick up the big flaws and active surface changes, don't you?" He stared at the Major. "I mean, how can we tell what sort of a hole we may be moving into, unless we have a scout up ahead?"

"That's what we have the charts for," the Major said sharply.

"Charts! I'm talking about *detail* work. We don't need to worry about the major topography. It's the little faults you can't see on the pictures that can kill us." He tossed the charts down excitedly. "Look, let me take a Bug out ahead and work reconnaissance, keep five, maybe ten miles ahead of the column. I can stay on good solid ground, of course, but scan the area closely and radio back to Peter where to avoid the flaws. Then—"

"No dice," the Major broke in.

"But why not? We could save ourselves days!"

"I don't care what we could save. We stay together. When we get to the Center, I want live men along with me. That means we stay within easy sight of each other at all times. Any climber knows that everybody is safer in a party than one man alone—any time, any place."

McIvers stared at him, his cheeks an angry red. Finally he gave a sullen nod. "Okay. If you say so."

"Well, I say so and I mean it. I don't want any fancy stuff. We're going to hit Center together, and finish the Crossing together. Got that?"

McIvers nodded. Mikuta then looked at Stone and me and we nodded, too.

"All right," he said slowly. "Now that we've got it straight, let's go."

It was hot. If I forget everything else about that trek, I'll never forget that huge yellow Sun glaring down, without a break, hotter and hotter with every mile. We knew that the first few days would be the easiest and we were rested and fresh when we started down the long ragged gorge southeast of the Twilight Lab.

I moved out first; back over my shoulder, I could see the Major and McIvers crawling out behind me, their pillow tires taking the rugged floor of the gorge smoothly. Behind them, Stone dragged the sledges.

Even at only 30 per cent Earth gravity they were a strain on the big tractor, until the ski-blades bit into the fluffy volcanic ash blanketing the valley. We even had a path to follow for the first twenty miles.

I kept my eyes pasted to the big polaroid binocs, picking out the track the early research teams had made out into the edge of Brightside. But in a couple of hours we rumbled past Sanderson's little outpost observatory and the tracks stopped. We were in virgin territory and already the Sun was beginning to bite.

We didn't *feel* the heat so much those first days out. We *saw* it. The refrig units kept our skins at a nice comfortable seventy-five degrees Fahrenheit inside our suits, but our eyes watched that glaring Sun and the baked yellow rocks going past, and some nerve pathways got twisted up, somehow. We poured sweat as if we were in a superheated furnace.

We drove eight hours and slept five. When a sleep period came due, we pulled the Bugs together into a square, threw up a light aluminum sun-shield and lay out in the dust and rocks. The sun-shield cut the temperature down sixty or seventy degrees, for whatever help that was. And then we ate from the forward sledge—sucking through tubes—protein, carbohydrates, bulk gelatin, vitamins.

The Major measured water out with an iron hand, because we'd have drunk ourselves into nephritis in a week otherwise. We were constantly, unceasingly thirsty. Ask the physiologists and psychiatrists why—they can give you have a dozen interesting reasons—but all we knew, or cared about, was that it happened to be so.

We didn't sleep the first few stops, as a consequence. Our eyes burned in spite of the filters and we had roaring headaches, but we couldn't sleep them off. We sat around looking at each other. Then McIvers would say how good a beer would taste, and off we'd go. We'd have murdered our grandmothers for one ice-cold bottle of beer.

After a few driving periods, I began to get my bearings at the wheel. We were moving down into desolation that made Earth's old Death Valley look like a Japanese rose garden. Huge sun-baked cracks opened up in the floor of the gorge, with black cliffs jutting up on either side; the air was filled with a barely visible yellowish mist of sulfur and sulfurous gases.

It was a hot, barren hole, no place for any man to go, but the challenge was so powerful you could almost feel it. No one had ever crossed this land before and escaped. Those who had tried it had been cruelly punished, but the land was still there, so it had to be crossed. Not the easy way. It had to be crossed the hardest way possible: overland, through anything the land could throw up to us, at the most difficult time possible.

Yet we knew that even the land might have been conquered before, except for that Sun. We'd fought absolute cold before and won. We'd never fought heat like this and won. The only worse heat in the Solar System was the surface of the Sun itself.

Brightside was worth trying for. We would get it or it would get us. That was the bargain.

I learned a lot about Mercury those first few driving periods. The gorge petered out after a hundred miles and we moved onto the slope of a range of ragged craters that ran south and east. This range had shown no activity since the first landing on Mercury forty years before, but beyond it there were active cones. Yellow fumes rose from the craters constantly; their sides were shrouded with heavy ash.

We couldn't detect a wind, but we knew there was a hot, sulfurous breeze sweeping in great continental tides across the face of the planet. Not enough for erosion, though. The craters rose up out of jagged gorges, huge towering spears of rock and rubble. Below were the vast yellow flatlands, smoking and hissing from the gases beneath the crust. Over everything was gray dust—silicates and salts, pumice and limestone and granite ash, filling crevices and declivities—offering a soft, treacherous surface for the Bug's pillow tires.

I learned to read the ground, to tell a covered fault by the sag of the dust; I learned to spot a passable crack, and tell it from an impassable cut. Time after time the Bugs ground to a halt while we explored a passage on foot, tied together with light copper cable, digging, advancing, digging some more until we were sure the surface would carry the machines. It was cruel work; we slept in exhaustion. But it went smoothly, at first.

Too smoothly, it seemed to me, and the others seemed to think so, too.

McIvers' restlessness was beginning to grate on our nerves. He talked too much, while we were resting or while we were driving; wisecracks, witticisms, unfunny jokes that wore thin with repetition. He took to making side trips from the route now and then, never far, but a little further each time.

Jack Stone reacted quite the opposite; he grew quieter with each stop, more reserved and apprehensive. I didn't like it, but I figured that it would pass off after a while. I was apprehensive enough myself; I just managed to hide it better.

And every mile the Sun got bigger and whiter and higher in the sky and hotter. Without our ultra-violet screens and glare filters we would have been blinded; as it was our eyes ached constantly and the skin on our faces itched and tingled at the end of an eight-hour trek.

But it took one of those side trips of McIvers' to deliver the penultimate blow to our already fraying nerves. He had driven down a side-branch of a long canyon running off west of our route and was almost out of sight in a cloud of ash when we heard a sharp cry through our earphones.

I wheeled my Bug around with my heart in my throat and spotted him through the binocs, waving frantically from the top of his machine. The Major and I took off, lumbering down the gulch after him as fast as the Bugs could go, with a thousand horrible pictures racing through our minds. . . .

We found him standing stock-still, pointing down the gorge and, for once, he didn't have anything to say. It was the wreck of a Bug; an old-fashioned half-track model of the sort that hadn't been in use for years. It was wedged tight in a cut in the rock, an axle broken, its casing split wide open up the middle, half-buried in a rock slide. A dozen feet away were two insulated suits with white bones gleaming through the fiberglass helmets.

This was as far as Wyatt and Carpenter had gotten on *their* Brightside Crossing.

On the fifth driving period out, the terrain began to change. It looked the same, but every now and then it *felt* different. On two occasions I felt my wheels spin, with a howl of protest from my engine. Then, quite suddenly, the Bug gave a lurch; I gunned my motor and nothing happened.

I could see the dull gray stuff seeping up around the hubs, thick and tenacious, splattering around in steaming gobs as the wheels spun. I knew what had happened the moment the wheels gave and, a few minutes later, they chained me to the tractor and dragged me back out of the mire. It looked for all the world like thick gray mud, but it was a pit of molten lead, steaming under a soft layer of concealing ash.

I picked my way more cautiously then. We were getting into an area of recent surface activity; the surface was really treacherous. I caught myself wishing that the Major had okayed McIvers' scheme for an advanced scout; more dangerous for the individual, maybe, but I was driving blind now and I didn't like it.

One error in judgment could sink us all, but I wasn't thinking much about the others. I was worried about *me,* plenty worried. I kept thinking, better McIvers should go than me. It wasn't healthy thinking and I knew it, but I couldn't get the thought out of my mind.

It was a grueling eight hours and we slept poorly. Back in the Bug again, we moved still more slowly—edging out on a broad flat plateau, dodging a network of gaping surface cracks—winding back and forth in an effort to keep the machines on solid rock. I couldn't see far ahead, because of the yellow haze rising from the cracks, so I was almost on top of it when I saw a sharp cut ahead where the surface dropped six feet beyond a deep crack.

I let out a shout to halt the others; then I edged my Bug forward, peering at the cleft. It was deep and wide. I moved fifty yards to the left, then back to the right.

There was only one place that looked like a possible crossing; a long, narrow ledge of gray stuff that lay down across a section of the fault like a ramp. Even as I watched it, I could feel the surface crust under the Bug trembling and saw the ledge shift over a few feet.

The Major's voice sounded in my ears. "How about it, Peter?"

"I don't know. This crust is on roller skates," I called back. "How about that ledge?"

I hesitated. "I'm scared of it, Major. Let's backtrack and try to find a way around."

There was a roar of disgust in my earphones and McIvers' Bug suddenly lurched forward. It rolled down past me, picked up speed, with McIvers hunched behind the wheel like a race driver. He was heading past me straight for the gray ledge.

My shout caught in my throat; I heard the Major take a huge breath and roar: "Mac! *stop that thing,* you fool!" and then McIvers' Bug was out on the ledge, lumbering across like a juggernaut.

The ledge jolted as the tires struck it; for a horrible moment, it seemed to be sliding out from under the machine. And then the Bug was across in a cloud of dust, and I heard McIvers' voice in my ears, shouting in glee. "Come on, you slowpokes. It'll hold you!"

Something unprintable came through the earphones as the Major drew up alongside me and moved his Bug out on the ledge slowly and over to the other side. Then he said, "Take it slow, Peter. Then give Jack a hand with the sledges." His voice sounded tight as a wire.

Ten minutes later, we were on the other side of the cleft. The Major checked the whole column; then he turned on McIvers angrily. "One more trick like that," he said, "and I'll strap you to a rock and leave you. Do you understand me? *One more time—*"

McIvers' voice was heavy with protest. "Good Lord, if we leave it up to Claney, he'll have us out here forever! Any blind fool could see that that ledge would hold."

"*I* saw it moving," I shot back at him.

"All right, all right, so you've got good eyes. Why all the fuss? We got across, didn't we? But I say we've got to have a little nerve and use it once in a while if we're ever going to get across this lousy hotbox."

"We need to use a little judgment, too," the Major snapped. "All right, let's roll. But if you think I was joking, you just try me out once." He let it soak in for a minute. Then he geared his Bug on around to my flank again.

At the stopover, the incident wasn't mentioned again, but the Major drew me aside just as I was settling down for sleep. "Peter, I'm worried," he said slowly.

"McIvers? Don't worry. He's not as reckless as he seems—just impatient. We are over a hundred miles behind schedule and we're moving awfully slow. We only made forty miles this last drive."

The Major shook his head. "I don't mean McIvers. I mean the kid."

"Jack? What about him?"

"Take a look."

Stone was shaking. He was over near the tractor—away from the rest of us—and he was lying on his back, but he wasn't asleep. His whole body was shaking, convulsively. I saw him grip an outcropping of rock hard.

I walked over and sat down beside him. "Get your water all right?" I said.

He didn't answer. He just kept on shaking.

"Hey, boy," I said. "What's the trouble?"

"It's hot," he said, choking out the words.

"Sure it's hot, but don't let it throw you. We're in really good shape."

"*We're not,*" he snapped. "We're in rotten shape, if you ask me. *We're not going to make it,* do you know that? That crazy fool's going to kill us for sure—" All of a sudden, he was bawling like a baby. "I'm scared—I shouldn't be here—I'm *scared*. What am I trying to prove by coming out here, for God's sake? I'm some kind of hero or something? I tell you I'm scared—"

"Look," I said. "Mikuta's scared, *I'm* scared. So what? We'll make it, don't worry. And nobody's trying to be a hero."

"Nobody but Hero Stone," he said bitterly. He shook himself and gave a tight little laugh. "Some hero, eh?"

"We'll make it," I said.

"Sure," he said finally. "Sorry. I'll be okay."

I rolled over, but waited until he was good and quiet.Then I tried to sleep, but I didn't sleep too well. I kept thinking about that ledge. I'd known from the look of it what it was; a zinc slough of the sort Sanderson had warned us about, a wide sheet of almost pure zinc that had been thrown up white-hot from below, quite recently, just waiting for oxygen or sulfur to rot it through.

I knew enough about zinc to know that at these temperatures it gets brittle as glass. Take a chance like McIvers had taken and the whole sheet could snap like a dry pine board. And it wasn't McIvers' fault that it hadn't.

Five hours later, we were back at the wheel. We were hardly moving at all. The ragged surface was almost impassable—great jutting rocks peppered the plateau; ledges crumbled the moment my tires touched them; long, open canyons turned into lead-mires or sulfur pits.

A dozen times I climbed out of the Bug to prod out an uncertain area with my boots and pikestaff. Whenever I did, McIvers piled out behind me, running ahead like a schoolboy at the fair, then climbing back again red-faced and panting, while we moved the machines ahead another mile or two.

Time was pressing us now and McIvers wouldn't let me forget it. We had made only about three hundred twenty miles in six driving periods, so we were about a hundred miles or even more behind schedule.

"We're not going to make it," McIvers would complain angrily. "That Sun's going to be out to aphelion by the time we hit the Center—"

"Sorry, but I can't take it any faster," I told him. I was getting good and mad. I knew what he wanted, but didn't dare let him have it. I was scared enough pushing the Bug out on those ledges, even knowing that at least *I* was making the decisions. Put him in the lead and we wouldn't last for eight hours. Our nerves wouldn't take it, at any rate, even if the machines would.

Jack Stone looked up from the aluminum chart sheets. "Another hundred miles and we should hit a good stretch," he said. "Maybe we can make up distance there for a couple of days."

The Major agreed, but McIvers couldn't hold his impatience. He kept staring up at the Sun as if he had a personal grudge against it and stamped back and forth under the sunshield. "That'll be just fine," he said. "*If* we ever get that far, that is."

We dropped it there, but the Major stopped me as we climbed aboard for the next run. "That guy's going to blow wide open if we don't move faster, Peter. I don't want him in the lead, no matter what happens. He's right though, about the need to make better time. Keep your head, but crowd your luck a little, okay?"

"I'll try," I said. It was asking the impossible and Mikuta knew it. We were on a long downward slope that shifted and buckled all around us, as though there were a molten underlay beneath the crust; the slope was broken by huge crevasses, partly covered with dust and zinc sheeting, like a vast glacier of stone and metal. The outside temperature registered 547° F. and getting hotter. It was no place to start rushing ahead.

I tried it anyway. I took half a dozen shaky passages, edging slowly out on flat zinc ledges, then toppling over and across. It seemed easy for a while and we made progress. We hit an even stretch and raced ahead. And then I quickly jumped on my brakes and jerked the Bug to a halt in a cloud of dust.

I'd gone too far. We were out on a wide, flat sheet of gray stuff, apparently solid—until I'd suddenly caught sight of the crevasse beneath in the corner of my eye. It was an overhanging shell that trembled under me as I stopped.

McIvers' voice was in my ear. "What's the trouble now, Claney?"

"Move back!" I shouted. "It can't hold us!"

"Looks solid enough from here."

"You want to argue about it? It's too thin, it'll snap. Move back!"

I started edging back down the ledge. I heard McIvers swear; then I saw his Bug start to creep *outward* on the shelf. Not fast or reckless, this time, but slowly, churning up dust in a gentle cloud behind him.

I just stared and felt the blood rush to my head. It seemed so hot I could hardly breathe as he edged out beyond me, further and further—

I think I felt it snap before I saw it. My own machine gave a sickening lurch and a long black crack appeared across the shelf—and widened. Then the ledge began to upend. I heard a scream as McIvers' Bug rose up and up and then crashed down into the crevasse in a thundering slide of rock and shattered metal.

I just stared for a full minute, I think. I couldn't move until I heard Jack Stone groan and the Major shouting, "Claney! I couldn't see—what *happened?*"

"It snapped on him, that's what happened," I roared. I gunned my motor, edged forward toward the fresh broken edge of the shelf. The crevasse gaped; I couldn't see any sign of the machine. Dust was still billowing up blindingly from below.

We stood staring down, the three of us. I caught a glimpse of Jack Stone's face through his helmet. It wasn't pretty.

"Well," said the Major heavily, "that's that."

"I guess so." I felt the way Stone looked.

"Wait," said Stone. "I heard something."

He had. It was a cry in the earphones—faint, but unmistakable.

"Mac!" The Major called. "Mac, can you hear me?"

"Yeah, yeah. I can hear you." The voice was very weak.

"Are you all right?"

"I don't know. Broken leg, I think. It's—hot." There was a long pause. Then: "I think my cooler's gone out."

The Major shot me a glance, then turned to Stone. "Get a cable from the second sledge fast. He'll fry alive if we don't get him out of there. Peter, I need you to lower me. Use the tractor winch."

I lowered him; he stayed down only a few moments. When I hauled him up, his face was drawn. "Still alive," he panted. "He won't be very long, though." He hesitated for just an instant. "We've got to make a try."

"I don't like this ledge," I said. "It's moved twice since I got out. Why not back off and lower him a cable?"

"No good. The Bug is smashed and he's inside it. We'll need

torches and I'll need one of you to help." He looked at me and then gave Stone a long look. "Peter, you'd better come."

"Wait," said Stone. His face was very white. "Let me go down with you."

"Peter is lighter."

"I'm not so heavy. Let me go down."

"Okay, if that's the way you want it." The Major tossed him a torch. "Peter, check these hitches and lower us slowly. If you see any kind of trouble, *anything,* cast yourself free and back off this thing, do you understand? This whole ledge may go."

I nodded. "Good luck."

They went over the ledge. I let the cable down bit by bit until it hit two hundred feet and slacked off.

"How does it look?" I shouted.

"Bad," said the Major. "We'll have to work fast. This whole side of the crevasse is ready to crumble. Down a little more."

Minutes passed without a sound. I tried to relax, but I couldn't. Then I felt the ground shift, and the tractor lurched to the side.

The Major shouted, *"It's going, Peter—pull back!"* and I threw the tractor into reverse, jerked the controls as the tractor rumbled off the shelf. The cable snapped, coiled up in front like a broken clockspring. The whole surface under me was shaking wildly now; ash rose in huge gray clouds. Then, with a roar, the whole shelf lurched and slid sideways. It teetered on the edge for seconds before it crashed into the crevasse, tearing the side wall down with it in a mammoth slide. I jerked the tractor to a halt as the dust and flame billowed up.

They were gone—all three of them, McIvers and the Major and Jack Stone—buried under a thousand tons of rock and zinc and molten lead. There wasn't any danger of anybody ever finding their bones.

Peter Claney leaned back, finishing his drink, rubbing his scarred face as he looked across at Baron.

Slowly, Baron's grip relaxed on the chair arm. "*You* got back," he said.

Claney nodded. "I got back, sure. I had the tractor and the sledges. I had seven days to drive back under that yellow Sun. I had plenty of time to think."

"You took the wrong man along," Baron said. "That was your mistake. Without him you would have made it."

"Never." Claney shook his head. "That's what I was thinking the first day or so—that it was *McIvers'* fault, that *he* was to blame. But that isn't true. He was wild, reckless and had lots of nerve."

"But his judgment was bad!"

"It couldn't have been sounder. We had to keep to our schedule even if it killed us, because it would positively kill us if we didn't."

"But a man like that—"

"A man like McIvers was necessary. Can't you see that? It was the Sun that beat us, that surface. Perhaps we were licked the very day we started." Claney leaned across the table, his eyes pleading. "We didn't realize that, but it was *true*. There are places that men can't go, conditions men can't tolerate. The others had to die to learn that. I was lucky, I came back. But I'm trying to tell you what I found out—that *nobody* will ever make a Brightside Crossing."

"We will," said Baron. "It won't be a picnic, but we'll make it."

"But suppose you do," said Claney, suddenly. "Suppose I'm all wrong, suppose you *do* make it. Then what? *What comes next?*"

"The Sun," said Baron.

Claney nodded slowly. "Yes. That would be it, wouldn't it?" He laughed. "Good-by, Baron. Jolly talk and all that. Thanks for listening."

Baron caught his wrist as he started to rise. "Just one question more, Claney. Why did you come here?"

"To try to talk you out of killing yourself," said Claney.

"You're a liar," said Baron.

Claney stared down at him for a long moment. Then he crumpled in the chair. There was defeat in his pale blue eyes and something else.

"Well?"

Peter Claney spread his hands, a helpless gesture. "When do you leave, Baron? I want you to take me along."

The Native Soil

BEFORE the first ship from Earth made a landing on Venus, there was much speculation about what might be found beneath the cloud layers obscuring that planet's surface from the eyes of all observers.

One school of thought maintained that the surface of Venus was a jungle, rank with hot-house moisture, crawling with writhing fauna and man-eating flowers. Another group contended hotly that Venus was an arid desert of wind-carved sandstone, dry and cruel, whipping dust into clouds that sunlight could never penetrate. Others prognosticated an ocean planet with little or no solid ground at all, populated by enormous serpents waiting to greet the first Earthlings with jaws agape.

But nobody knew, of course. Venus was the planet of mystery.

When the first Earth ship finally landed there, all they found was a great quantity of mud.

There was enough mud on Venus to go all the way around twice, with some left over. It was warm, wet, soggy mud—clinging and tenacious. In some places it was gray, and in other places it was black. Elsewhere it was found to be varying shades of brown, yellow, green, blue and purple. But just the same, it was still mud. The sparse Venusian vegetation grew up out of it; the small Venusian natives lived down in it; the steam rose from it and the rain fell on it, and that, it seemed, was that. The planet of mystery was no longer mysterious. It was just messy. People didn't talk about it any more.

But technologists of the Piper Pharmaceuticals, Inc., R&D squad found a certain charm in the Venusian mud.

They began sending cautious and very secret reports back to the Home Office when they discovered just what, exactly was growing in that Venusian mud besides Venusian natives. The Home Office promptly bought up full exploratory and mining rights to the planet for a price that was a brazen steal, and then in high excitement began pouring millions of dollars into ships and machines bound for the muddy planet. The Board of Directors met hoots of derision with secret smiles as they rubbed their hands together softly. Special crews of psychologists were dispatched to Venus to contact the natives; they returned, exuberant, with test-results that proved the natives were friendly, intelligent, co-operative and resourceful, and the Board of Directors rubbed their hands more eagerly together, and poured more money into the Piper Venusian Installation.

It took money to make money, they thought. Let the fools laugh. They wouldn't be laughing long. After all, Piper Pharmaceuticals, Inc., could recognize a gold mine when they saw one.

They thought.

Robert Kielland, special investigator and trouble shooter for Piper Pharmaceuticals, Inc., made an abrupt and intimate acquaintance with the fabulous Venusian mud when the landing craft brought him down on that soggy planet. He had transferred from the great bubble-shaped orbital transport ship to the sleek landing craft an hour before, bored and impatient with the whole proposition. He had no desire whatever to go to Venus. He didn't like mud, and he didn't like frontier projects. There had been nothing in his contract with Piper demanding that he travel to other planets in pursuit of his duties, and he had balked at the assignment. He had even balked at the staggering bonus check they offered him to help him get used to the idea.

It was not until they had convinced him that only his own superior judgment, his razor-sharp mind and his extraordinarily shrewd powers of observation and insight could possibly pull Piper Pharmaceuticals, Inc., out of the mudhole they'd gotten themselves into, that he had reluctantly agreed to go. He wouldn't like a moment of it, but he'd go.

Things weren't going right on Venus, it seemed.

The trouble was that millions were going in and nothing was coming out. The early promise of high production figures had faltered, sagged, dwindled and vanished. Venus was getting to be an expensive project to have around, and nobody seemed to know just why.

Now the pilot dipped the landing craft in and out of the cloud blanket, braking the ship, falling closer and closer to the surface as Kielland watched gloomily from the after port. The lurching billows of clouds made him queasy; he opened his Piper samples case and popped a pill into his mouth. Then he gave his nose a squirt or two with his Piper Rhino-Vac nebulizer, just for good measure. Finally, far below them, the featureless gray surface skimmed by. A sparse scraggly forest of twisted gray foliage sprang up at them.

The pilot sighted the landing platform, checked with Control Tower, and eased up for the final descent. He was a skillful pilot, with many landings on Venus to his credit. He brought the ship up on its tail and sat it down on the landing platform for a perfect three-pointer as the jets rumbled to silence.

Then, abruptly, they sank—landing craft, platform and all.

The pilot buzzed Control Tower frantically as Kielland fought down panic. Sorry, said Control Tower. Something must have gone wrong. They'd have them out in a jiffy. Good lord, no, *don't* blast out again, there were a thousand natives in the vicinity. Just be patient, everything would be all right.

They waited. Presently there were thumps and bangs as grapplers clanged on the surface of the craft. Mud gurgled around them as they were hauled up and out with the sound of a giant sipping soup. A mud-encrusted hatchway flew open, and Kielland stepped down on a flimsy-looking platform below. Four small rodent-like creatures were attached to it by ropes; they heaved with a will and began paddling through the soupy mud dragging the platform and Kielland toward a row of low wooden buildings near some stunted trees.

As the creatures paused to puff and pant, the back half of the platform kept sinking into the mud. When they finally reached comparatively solid ground, Kielland was mud up to the hips, and mad enough to blast off without benefit of landing craft.

He surveyed the Piper Venusian Installation, hardly believing what he saw. He had heard the glowing descriptions of the Board of Directors. He had seen the architect's projections of fine modern buildings resting on water-proof buoys, neat boating channels to the mine sites, fine orange-painted dredge equipment (including the new Piper Axis-Traction Dredges that had been developed especially for the operation). It had sounded, in short, just the way a Piper Installation ought to sound.

But there was nothing here that resembled that. Kielland could see a group of little wooden shacks that looked as though they were ready at a moment's notice to sink with a gurgle into the mud. Off to the right across a mud flat one of the dredges apparently had done just that: a swarm of men and natives were hard at work dragging it up again. Control Tower was to the left, balanced precariously at a slight tilt in a sea of mud.

The Piper Venusian Installation didn't look too much like a going concern. It looked far more like a ghost town in the latter stages of decay.

Inside the Administration shack Kielland found a weary-looking man behind a desk, scribbling furiously at a pile of reports. Everything in the shack was splattered with mud. The crude desk and furniture was smeared; the papers had black speckles all over them. Even the man's face was splattered, his clothing encrusted with gobs of still-damp mud. In a corner a young man was industriously scrubbing down the wall with a large brush.

The man wiped mud off Kielland and jumped up with a gleam of hope in his tired eyes. "Ah! Wonderful!" he cried. "Great to see you, old man. You'll find all the papers and reports in order here, everything ready for you—" He brushed the papers away from him with a gesture of finality. "Louie, get the landing craft pilot and don't let him out of your sight. Tell him I'll be ready in twenty minutes—"

"Hold it," said Kielland. "Aren't you Simpson?"

The man wiped mud off his cheeks and spat. He was tall and graying. "That's right."

"Where do you think you're going?"

"Aren't you relieving me?"

"I am not!"

"Oh, my." The man crumbled behind the desk, as though his legs had just given way. "I don't understand it. They told me—"

"I don't care what they told you," said Kielland shortly. "I'm a trouble shooter, not an administrator. When production figures begin to drop, I find out why. The production figures from this place have never gotten high enough to drop."

"This is supposed to be news to me?" said Simpson.

"So you've got troubles."

"Friend, you're right about that."

"Well, we'll straighten them out," Kielland said smoothly. "But first I want to see the foreman who put that wretched landing platform together."

Simpson's eyes became wary. "Uh—you don't really want to see him?"

"Yes, I think I do. When there's such obvious evidence of incompetence, the time to correct it is now."

"Well—maybe we can go outside and see him."

"We'll see him right here." Kielland sank down on the bench near the wall. A tiny headache was developing; he found a capsule in his samples case and popped it in his mouth.

Simpson looked sad and nodded to the orderly who had stopped scrubbing down the wall. "Louie, you heard the man."

"But boss—"

Simpson scowled. Louie went to the door and whistled. Presently there was a splashing sound and a short, gray creature padded in. His hind feet were four-toed webbed paddles; his legs were long and powerful like a kangaroo's. He was covered with thick gray fur which dripped with thick black mud. He squeaked at Simpson, wriggling his nose. Simpson squeaked back sharply.

Suddenly the creature began shaking his head in a slow, rhythmic undulation. With a cry Simpson dropped behind the desk. The orderly fell flat on the floor, covering his face with his arm. Kielland's eyes widened; then he was sitting in a deluge of mud as the little Venusian shook himself until his fur stood straight out in all directions.

Simpson stood up again with a roar. "I've told them a thousand times if I've told them once—" He shook his head helplessly as Kielland wiped mud out of his eyes. "This is the one you wanted to see."

Kielland sputtered. "Can it talk to you?"

"It doesn't talk, it squeaks."

"Then ask it to explain why the platform it built didn't hold the landing craft."

Simpson began whistling and squeaking at length to the little creature. Its shaggy tail crept between its legs and it hung its head like a scolded puppy.

"He says he didn't know a landing craft was supposed to land on the platform," Simpson reported finally. "He's sorry, he says."

"But hasn't he seen a landing craft before?"

Squeak, squeak. "Oh, yes."

"Wasn't he told what the platform was being made for?"

Squeak, squeak. "Of course."

"Then why didn't the platform stand up?"

Simpson sighed. "Maybe he forgot what it was supposed to be used for in the course of building it. Maybe he never really did understand in the first place. I can't get questions like that across to him with this whistling, and I doubt that you'll ever find out which it was."

"Then fire him," said Kielland. "We'll find some other—"

"Oh, no! I mean, let's not be hasty," said Simpson. "I'd hate to have to fire this one—for a while yet, at any rate."

"Why?"

"Because we've finally gotten across to him—at least I *think* we have—just how to take down a dredge tube." Simpson's voice was almost tearful. "It's taken us months to teach him. If we fire him, we'll have to start all over again with another one."

Kielland stared at the Venusian, and then at Simpson. "So," he said finally, "I see."

"No, you don't," Simpson said with conviction. "You don't even begin to see yet. You have to fight it for a few months before you really see." He waved the Venusian out the door and turned to Kielland with burden of ten months' frustration in his voice. "They're *stupid*," he said slowly. "They are so incredibly stupid I could go screaming into the swamp every time I see one of them coming. Their stupidity is positively abysmal."

"Then why use them?" Kielland spluttered.

"Because if we ever hope to mine anything in this miserable mudhole, we've got to use them to do it. There just isn't any other way."

With Simpson leading, they donned waist-high waders with wide, flat silicone-coated pans strapped to the feet and started out to inspect the installation.

A crowd of a dozen or more Venusian natives swarmed happily around them like a pack of hounds. They were in and out of the steaming mud, circling and splashing, squeaking and shaking. They seemed to be having a real field day.

"Of course," Simpson was saying, "since Number Four dredge sank last week there isn't a whale of a lot of Installation left for you to inspect. But you can see what there is, if you want."

"You mean Number Four dredge is the only one you've got to use?" Kielland asked peevishly. "According to my records you have five Axis-Traction dredges, plus a dozen or more of the old kind."

"Ah!" said Simpson. "Well, Number One had its vacuum chamber corroded out a week after we started using dredging. Ran into a vein of stuff with 15 per cent acid content, and it got chewed up something fierce. Number Two sank without a trace—over there in the swamp someplace." He pointed across the black mud flats to a patch of sickly vegetation. "The Mud-pups know where it is, they think, and I suppose they could go drag it up for us if we dared take the time, but it would lose us a month, and you know the production schedule we've been trying to meet."

"So what about Numbers Three and Five?"

"Oh, we still have them. They won't work without a major overhaul, though."

"Overhaul! They're brand new."

"They *were*. The Mud-pups didn't understand how to sluice them down properly after operations. When this guck gets out into the air it hardens like cement. You ever see a cement mixer that hasn't been cleaned out after use for a few dozen times? That's Numbers Three and Five."

"What about the old style models?"

"Half of them are out of commission, and the other half are holding the islands still."

"Islands?"

"Those chunks of semisolid ground we have Administration built on. The chunk that keeps Control Tower in one place."

"Well, what are they going to do—walk away?"

"That's just about right. The first week we were in operation we kept wondering why we had to travel farther every day to get to the dredges. Then we realized that solid ground on Venus isn't solid ground at all. It's just big chunks of denser stuff that floats on top of the mud like dumplings in a stew. But that was nothing compared to the other things—"

They had reached the vicinity of the salvage operation on Number Five dredge. To Kielland it looked like a huge cylinder-type vacuum cleaner with a number of flexible hoses sprouting from the top. The whole machine was three-quarters submerged in clinging mud. Off to the right a derrick floated hub-deep in slime; grapplers from it were clinging to the dredge and the derrick was heaving and splashing like a trapped hippopotamus. All about the submerged machine were Mud-pups, working like strange little beavers as the man supervising the operation wiped mud from his face and carried on a running line of shouts, curses, whistles and squeaks.

Suddenly one of the Mud-pups saw the newcomers. He let out a squeal, dropped his line in the mud and bounced up to the surface, dancing like a dervish on his broad webbed feet as he stared in unabashed curiosity. A dozen more followed his lead, squirming up and staring, shaking gobs of mud from their fur.

"No, *no!*" the man supervising the operation screamed. "*Pull,* you idiots. Come back here! Watch *out*—"

The derrick wobbled and let out a whine as steel cable sizzled out. Confused, the Mud-pups tore themselves away from the newcomers and turned back to their lines, but it was too late. Number Five dredge trembled, with a wet sucking sound, and settled back into the mud, blub—blub—blub.

The supervisor crawled down from his platform and sloshed across to where Simpson and Kielland were standing. He looked like a man who had suffered the torment of the damned for twenty minutes too long. "No more!" he screamed in Simpson's face. "That's all. I'm through. I'll pick up my pay any time you get it ready, and I'll finish off my contract at home, but I'm through here. One solid week I work to teach these idiots what I want them to do, and you have to come along at the one moment all week when I really need their concentration." He glared, his face purple. "Concentration! I should hope for so much! You got to have a brain to have concentration—"

"Barton, this is Kielland. He's here from the Home Office, to solve all our problems."

"You mean he brought us an evacuation ship?"

"No, he's going to tell us how to make this Installation pay. Right, Kielland?" Simpson's grin was something to see.

Kielland scowled. "What are you going to do with the dredge—just leave it there?" he asked angrily.

"No—I'm going to dig it out, again," said Barton, "after we take another week off to drum into those quarter-brained mud-hens just what it is we want them to do—again—and then persuade them to do it—again—and then hope against hope that nothing happens along to distract them—again. Any suggestions?"

Simpson shook his head. "Take a rest, Barton. Things will look brighter in the morning."

"Nothing ever looks brighter in the morning," said Barton, and he sloshed angrily off toward the Administration island.

"You see?" said Simpson. "Or do you want to look around some more?"

Back in Administration shack, Kielland sprayed his throat with Piper Fortified Bio-Static and took two tetracycline capsules from his samples case as he stared gloomily down at the little gob of blue-gray mud on the desk before him.

The Venusian bonanza, the sole object of the multi-million-dollar Piper Venusian Installation, didn't look like much. It ran in veins deep beneath the surface. The R&D men had struck it quite by accident in the first place, sampled it along with a dozen other kinds of Venusian mud—and found they had their hands on the richest 'mycin-bearing bacterial growth since the days of the New Jersey mud flats.

The value of the stuff was incalculable. Twenty-first century Earth had not realized the degree to which it depended upon its effective antibiotic products for maintenance of its health until the mutating immune bacterial strains began to outpace the development of new antibacterials. Early penicillin killed 96 per cent of all organisms in its spectrum—at first—but time and natural selection undid its work in three generations. Even the broad-spectrum drugs were losing their effectiveness to a dangerous degree within decades of their introduction. And the new drugs grown from Earth-born bacteria, or synthesized in the laboratories, were too few and too weak to meet the burgeoning demands of humanity—

Until Venus. The bacteria indigenous to that planet were alien to Earth—every attempt to transplant them had failed—but they grew with abandon in the warm mud currents of Venus. Not all mud was of value: only the singular blue-gray stuff that lay before Kielland on the desk could produce the 'mycin-like tetracycline derivative that was more powerful than the best of Earth-grown wide spectrum antibiotics, with few if any of the unfortunate side-effects of the Earth products.

The problem seemed simple: find the mud in sufficient quantities for mining, dredge it up, and transport it back to Earth to extract the drug. It was the first two steps of the operation that depended so heavily on the mud-acclimated natives of Venus for success. They were as much at home in the mud as they were in the dank, humid air above. They could distinguish one type of mud from another deep beneath the surface, and could carry a dredge-tube down to a lode of the blue-gray muck with the unfailing accurary of a homing pigeon.

If they could only be made to understand just what they were expected to do. And that was where production ground down to a slow walk.

The next few days were a nightmare of frustration for Kielland as he observed with mounting horror the standard operating procedure of the Installation.

Men and Mud-pups went to work once again to drag Number Five dredge out of the mud. It took five days of explaining, repeating, coaxing and threatening to do it, but finally up it came—with mud caked and hardened in its insides until it could never be used again.

So they ferried Number Six down piecemeal from the special orbital transport ship that had brought it. Only three landing craft sank during the process, and within two weeks Simpson and Barton set bravely off with their dull-witted cohorts to tackle the swamp with a spanking new piece of equipment. At last the delays were over—

Of course, it took another week to get the actual dredging started. The Mud-pups who had been taught the excavation procedure previously had either disappeared into the swamp or forgotten everything they'd ever been taught. Simpson had expected it, but it was enough to keep Kielland sleepless for three nights and drive his blood pressure to suicidal levels. At length, the blue-gray mud began billowing out of the dredge onto the platforms built to receive it, and the transport ship was notified to stand by for loading. But by the time the ferry had landed, the platform with the load had somehow drifted free of the island and required a week-long expedition into the hinterland to track it down. On the trip back they met a rainstorm that dissolved the blue-gray stuff into soup which ran out between the slats of the platform, and back into the mud again. They did get the platform back, at any rate.

Meanwhile, the dredge began sucking up green stuff that smelled of sewage instead of the blue-gray clay they sought—so the natives dove mud-ward to explore the direction of the vein. One of them got caught in the suction tube, causing a three-day delay while engineers dismantled the dredge to get him out. In re-assembling, two of the dredge tubes got interlocked somehow, and the dredge burned out three generators trying to suck itself through itself, so to speak. That took another week to fix.

Kielland buried himself in the Administration shack, digging through the records, when the reign of confusion outside became too much to bear. He sent for Tarnier, the Installation physician, biologist, and erstwhile Venusian psychologist. Dr. Tarnier looked like the breathing soul of failure; Kielland had to steel himself to the wave of pity that swept through him at the sight of the man. "You're the one who tested these imbeciles originally?" he demanded.

Dr. Tarnier nodded. His face was seamed, his eyes lustreless. "I tested 'em. God help me, I tested 'em."

"How?"

"Standard procedures. Reaction times. Mazes. Conditioning. Language. Abstractions. Numbers. Associations. The works."

"Standard for Earthmen, I presume you mean."

"So what else? Piper didn't want to know if they were Einsteins or not. All they wanted was a passable level of intelligence. Give them natives with brains and they might have to pay them something. They thought they were getting a bargain."

"Some bargain."

"Yeah."

"Only your tests say they're intelligent. As intelligent, say, as a low-normal human being without benefit of any schooling or education. Right?"

"That's right," the doctor said wearily, as though he had been through this mill again and again. "Schooling and education don't enter into it at all, of course. All we measured was potential. But the results said they had it."

"Then how do you explain the mess we've got out there?"

"The tests were wrong. Or else they weren't applicable even on a basic level. Or something. I don't know. I don't even care much any more."

"Well I care, plenty. Do you realize how much those creatures are costing us? If we ever do get the finished product on the market, it'll cost too much for anybody to buy."

Dr. Tarnier spread his hands. "Don't blame me. Blame them."

"And then this so-called biological survey of yours," Kielland continued, warming to his subject. "From a scientific man, it's a prize. Anatomical description: limited because of absence of autopsy specimens. Apparently have endoskeleton, but organization of the internal organs remains obscure. Thought to be mammalianoid—there's a fence-sitter for you—but can't be certain of this because no young have been observed, nor any females in gestation. Extremely gregarious, curious, playful, irresponsible, etc., etc., etc. Habitat under natural conditions: uncertain. Diet: uncertain. Social organization: uncertain." Kielland threw down the paper with a snort. "In short, the only thing we're certain of is that they're here.

Very helpful. Especially when every dime we have in this project depends on our teaching them how to count to three without help."

Dr. Tarnier spread his hands again. "Mr. Kielland, I'm a mere mortal. In order to measure something, it has to stay the same long enough to get it measured. In order to describe something, it has to hold still long enough to be observed. In order to form a logical opinion of a creature's mental capacity, it has to demonstrate some perceptible mental capacity to start with. You can't get very far studying a creature's habitat and social structure when most of its habitating goes on under twenty feet of mud."

"How about the language?"

"We get by with squeaks and whistles and sign language. A sort of pidgeon-Venusian. They use a very complex system among themselves." The doctor paused, uncertainly. "Anyway, it's hard to get too tough with the Pups," he burst out finally. "They really seem to try hard—when they can just manage to keep their minds to it."

"Just stupid, carefree, happy-go-lucky kids, eh?"

Dr. Tarnier shrugged.

"Go away," said Kielland in disgust, and turned back to the reports with a sour taste in his mouth.

Later he called the Installation Comptroller. "What do you pay Mud-pups for their work?" he wanted to know.

"Nothing," said the Comptroller.

"Nothing!"

"We have nothing they can use. What would you give them —United Nations coin? They'd just try to eat it."

"How about something they *can* eat, then?"

"Everything we feed them they throw right back up. Planetary incompatibility."

"But there must be *something* you can use for wages," Kielland protested. "Something they want, something they'll work hard for."

"Well, they liked tobacco and pipes all right—but it interfered with their oxygen storage so they couldn't dive. That ruled out tobacco and pipes. They liked Turkish towels, too, but they spent all their time parading up and down in them and slaying the ladies and wouldn't work at all. That ruled out Turkish towels. They don't seem to care too much whether they're paid or not, though—as long as we're decent to them. They seem to like us, in a stupid sort of way."

"Just loving, affectionate, happy-go-lucky kids. I know. Go away." Kielland growled and turned back to the reports . . . except that there weren't any more reports that he hadn't read a dozen times or more. Nothing that made sense, nothing that offered a lead. Millions of Piper dollars sunk into this project, and every one of them sitting there blinking at him expectantly.

For the first time he wondered if there really *was* any solution to the problem. Stumbling blocks had been met and removed before—that was Kielland's job, and he knew how to do it. But stupidity could be a stumbling block that was all but insurmountable.

Yet he couldn't throw off the nagging conviction that something more subtle than stupidity was involved. . . .

Then Simpson came in, cursing and sputtering and bellowing for Louie. Louie came, and Simpson started dictating a message for relay to the transport ship. "Special order, rush, repeat, rush," Simpson grated. "For immediate delivery Piper Venusian Installation—one Piper Axis-Traction Dredge, previous specifications applicable—"

Kielland stared at him. "Again?"

Simpson gritted his teeth. "Again."

"Sunk?"

"Blub," said Simpson. "Blub, blub, blub."

Slowly, Kielland stood up, glaring first at Simpson, then at the little muddy creatures that were attempting to hide behind his waders, looking so forlorn and chastised and woebegone. "All right," Kielland said, after a pregnant pause. "That's all. You won't need to relay that order to the ship. Forget about Number Seven dredge. Just get your files in order and get a landing craft down here for me. The sooner the better."

Simpson's face lit up in pathetic eagerness. "You mean we're going to *leave?*"

"That's what I mean."

"The company's not going to like it—"

"The company ought to welcome us home with open arms," Kielland snarled. "They should shower us with kisses. They should do somersaults for joy that I'm not going to let them sink another half billion into the mud out here. They took a gamble and got cleaned, that's all. They'd be as stupid as your pals here if they kept coming back for more." He pulled on his waders, brushing penitent Mud-pups aside as he started for the door. "Send the natives back to their burrows or whatever they live in and get ready to close down. *I've* got to figure out some way to make a report to the Board that won't get us all fired."

He slammed out the door and started across to his quarters, waders going splat-splat in the mud. Half a dozen Mud-pups were following him. They seemed extraordinarily exuberant as they went diving and splashing in the mud. Kielland turned and roared at them, shaking his fist. They stopped short, then slunk off with their tails between their legs.

But even at that, their squeaking sounded strangely like laughter to Kielland. . . .

In his quarters the light was so dim that he almost had his waders off before he saw the upheaval. The little room was splattered from top to bottom with mud. His bunk was coated with slime; the walls dripped blue-gray goo. Across the room his wardrobe doors hung open as three muddy creatures rooted industriously in the leather case on the floor.

Kielland let out a howl and threw himself across the room. *His samples case!* The Mud-pups scattered, squealing. Their hands were filled with capsules, and their muzzles were dripping with white powder. Two went between Kielland's legs and through the door. The third dove for the window with Kielland after him. The company man's hand closed on a slippery tail, and he fell headlong across the muddy bed as the culprit literally slipped through his fingers.

He sat up, wiping mud from his hair and surveying the damage. Bottles and boxes of medicaments were scattered all over the floor of the wardrobe, covered with mud but unopened. Only one large box had been torn apart, its contents ravaged.

Kielland stared at it as things began clicking into place in his mind. He walked to the door, stared out across the steaming gloomy mud flats toward the lighted windows of the Administration shack. Sometimes, he mused, a man can get so close to something that he can't see the obvious. He stared at the samples case again. Sometimes stupidity works both ways—and sometimes what looks like stupidity may really be something far more deadly.

He licked his lips and flipped the telephone-talker switch. After a misconnection or two he got Control Tower. Control Tower said yes, they had a small exploratory scooter on hand. Yes, it could be controlled on a beam and fitted with cameras. But of course it was special equipment, emergency use only—

He cut them off and buzzed Simpson excitedly. "Cancel all

I said—about leaving. I mean. Change of plan. Something's come up. No, don't order anything—but get one of those natives that can understand your whistling and give him the word."

Simpson bellowed over the wire. "What word? What do you think you're doing?"

"I may just be saving our skins—we won't know for a while. But however you manage it, tell them we're definitely *not leaving Venus*. Tell them they're all fired—we don't want them around any more. The Installation is off limits to them from here on in. And tell them we've devised a way to mine the lode without them—got that? Tell them the equipment will be arriving as soon as we can bring it down from the transport."

"Oh, now look—"

"You want me to repeat it?"

Simpson sighed. "All right. Fine. I'll tell them. Then what?"

"Then just don't bother me for a while. I'm going to be busy. Watching TV."

An hour later Kielland was in Control Tower, watching the pale screen as the little remote-controlled explorer circled the installation. Three TV cameras were in operation as he settled down behind the screen. He told Sparks what he wanted to do, and the ship whizzed off in the direction the Mud-pup raiders had taken.

At first, there was nothing but dreary mud flats sliding past the cameras' watchful eyes. Then they picked up a flicker of movement, and the ship circled in lower for a better view. It was a group of natives—a large group. There must have been fifty of them working busily in the mud, five miles away from the Piper Installation. They didn't look so carefree and happy-go-lucky now. They looked very much like desperately busy

Mud-pups with a job on their hands, and they were so absorbed they didn't even see the small craft circling above them.

They worked in teams. Some were diving with small containers; some were handling lines attached to the containers; still others were carrying and dumping. They came up full, went down empty, came up full. The produce was heaped in a growing pile on a small semisolid island with a few scraggly trees on it. As they worked the pile grew and grew.

It took only a moment for Kielland to tell what they were doing. The color of the stuff was unmistakable. They were mining piles of blue-gray mud, just as fast as they could mine it.

With a gleam of satisfaction in his eye, Kielland snapped off the screen and nodded at Sparks to bring the cameras back. Then he rang Simpson again.

"Did you tell them?"

Simpson's voice was uneasy. "Yeah—yeah, I told them. They left in a hurry. Quite a hurry."

"Yes, I imagine they did. Where are your men now?"

"Out working on Number Six, trying to get it up."

"Better get them together and pack them over to Control Tower, fast," said Kielland. "I mean everybody. Every man in the Installation. We may have this thing just about tied up, if we can get out of here soon enough—"

Kielland's chair gave a sudden lurch and sailed across the room, smashing into the wall. With a yelp he tried to struggle up the sloping floor; it reared and heaved over the other way, throwing Kielland and Sparks to the other wall amid a heap of instruments. Through the windows they could see the gray mud flats careening wildly below them. It took only an instant to realize what was happening. Kielland shouted, "Let's get out of here!" and headed down the stairs, clinging to the railing for dear life.

Control Tower was sinking in the mud. They had moved faster than he had anticipated, Kielland thought, and snarled at himself all the way down to the landing platform below. He had hoped at least to have time to parley, to stop and discuss the whys and wherefores of the situation with the natives. Now it was abundantly clear that any whys and wherefores that were likely to be discussed would be discussed later.

And very possibly under twenty feet of mud—

A stream of men were floundering out of Administration shack, plowing through the mud with waders only half strapped on as the line of low buildings began shaking and sinking into the morass. From the direction of Number Six dredge another crew was heading for the Tower. But the Tower was rapidly growing shorter as the buoys that sustained it broke loose with ear-shattering crashes.

Kielland caught Sparks by the shoulder, shouting to be heard above the racket. "The transport—did you get it?"

"I—I think so."

"They're sending us a ferry?"

"It should be on its way."

Simpson sloshed up, his face heavy with dismay. "The dredges! They've cut loose the dredges."

"Bother the dredges. Get your men collected and into the shelters. We'll have a ship here any minute."

"But what's happening?"

"We're leaving—if we can make it before these carefree, happy-go-lucky kids here sink us in the mud, dredges, Control Tower and all."

Out of the gloom above there was a roar and a streak of murky yellow as the landing craft eased down through the haze. Only the top of Control Tower was out of the mud now. The Administration shack gave a lurch, sagging, as a dozen indistinct gray forms pulled and tugged at the supporting structure beneath it. Already a circle of natives was converging on the Earthmen as they gathered near the landing platform shelters.

"They're cutting loose the landing platform!" somebody wailed. One of the lines broke with a resounding snap, and the platform lurched. Then a dozen men dived through the mud to pull away the slippery, writhing natives as they worked to cut through the remaining guys. Moments later the landing craft was directly overhead and men and natives alike scattered as she sank down.

The platform splintered and jolted under her weight, began skidding, then held firm to the two guy ropes remaining. A horde of gray creatures hurled themselves on those lines as a hatchway opened above and a ladder dropped down. The men scurried up the ropes just as the plastic dome of the Control Tower sank with a gurgle.

Kielland and Simpson paused at the bottom of the ladder, blinking at the scene of devastation around them.

"Stupid, you say," said Kielland heavily. "Better get up there, or we'll go where Control Tower went."

"But—everything—gone!"

"Wrong again. Everything saved." Kielland urged the administrator up the ladder and sighed with relief as the hatch clanged shut. The jets bloomed and sprayed boiling mud far and wide as the landing craft lifted soggily out of the mire and roared for the clouds above.

Kielland wiped sweat from his forehead and sank back on his cot with a shudder. "*We* should be so stupid," he said.

"I must admit," he said later to a weary and mystified Simpson, "that I didn't expect them to move so fast. But when you've decided in your mind that somebody's really pretty stupid, it's hard to adjust to the idea that maybe he *isn't,* all of a sudden. We should have been much more suspicious of Dr. Tarnier's tests. It's true they weren't designed for Venusians, but they were designed to assess intelligence, and intelligence isn't a quality that's influenced by environment or species. It's either there or it isn't, and the good Doctor told us unequivocally that it was there."

"But their behavior."

"Even that should have tipped us off. There is a very fine line dividing incredible stupidity and incredible *stubbornness.* It's often a tough differential to make. I didn't spot it until I found them wolfing down the tetracycline capsules in my samples case. Then I began to see the implications. Those Mud-pups were stubbornly and tenaciously determined to drive the Piper Venusian Installation off Venus permanently, by fair means or foul. They didn't care how it got off—they just wanted it off."

"But why? We weren't hurting them. There's plenty of mud on Venus."

"Ah—but not so much of the blue-gray stuff we were after, perhaps. Suppose a space ship settled down in a wheatfield in Kansas along about harvest time and started loading wheat into the hold? I suppose the farmer wouldn't mind too much. After all, there's plenty of vegetation on Earth—"

"They're *growing* the stuff?"

"For all they're worth," said Kielland. "Lord knows what sort of metabolism uses tetracycline for food—but they are growing mud that yields an incredibly rich concentration of antibiotic . . . their native food. They grow it, harvest it, live on it. Even the way they shake whenever they come out of the mud is a giveaway—what better way to seed their crop far and wide? We were mining away their staff of life, my friend. You really couldn't blame them for objecting."

"Well, if they think they can drive us off that way, they're going to have to get that brilliant intelligence of theirs into action," Simpson said ominously. "We'll bring enough equipment down there to mine them out of house and home."

"Why?" said Kielland. "After all, they're mining it themselves a lot more efficiently than we could ever do it. And with Piper warehouses back on Earth full of old, useless antibiotics that they can't sell for peanuts? No, I don't think we'll mine anything when a simple trade arrangement will do just as well." He sank back in his cot, staring dreamily through the port as the huge orbital transport loomed large ahead of them. He found his throat spray and dosed himself liberally in preparation for his return to civilization. "Of course, the natives are going to be wondering what kind of idiots they're dealing with to sell them pure refined extract of Venusian beefsteak in return for raw chunks of unrefined native soil. But I think we can afford to just let them wonder for a while."

Love Thy Vimp

THE red "urgent" signal was blinking wildly on the library visiphone when Barney Holder walked into the house that evening. He glanced at it tiredly, then flipped his hat onto the shelf and called out, "I'm home, dear."

His wife looked up from her magazine with an owly stare. "So I see," she said indifferently, running a hand through her pretty blonde hair. "Only *two* hours late tonight. You're getting better all the time." She turned back to the magazine. "If you expect to eat tonight," she added, "you'll have to see what you can find. Your little friends got into the dinner."

"Oh, Flora!" Barney hesitated in the doorway, glancing uneasily at the blinking call-signal. "Really, dear, you might have waited until I got home—and covered the food so they couldn't get in." He stared at her unhappily.

"I suppose I should lock the dinner in a strongbox," Flora snapped angrily. "You're supposed to be getting rid of the nasty things, not feeding them." She tossed her head and glared at him as he started for the visiphone. "And it's about time you answered that thing, too. It's been blinking for half an hour."

Barney flipped the switch and watched the screen blink and

waver until Hugo Martin's broad face was clearly outlined. Barney's boss was normally large and florid of face; now his cheeks were almost purple, his eyes wide with excitement. "Barney!" he cried, *"we've got one!"*

Barney sat down abruptly, excitement rising in his chest. "You're kidding," he said quickly. "You mean we've—"

Martin nodded, almost incoherent. "We've got one! Right out in our own laboratory! It's sitting there snarling at me right now. You know that trap you built?"

"Oh, nonsense," Barney snapped. *"Nobody's* ever caught a Vimp. I've built fifty traps if I've built one, and not one of them ever worked." He stopped and looked at the florid face on the screen, his eyes bright. "Do you really mean it?"

"Of course I mean it! That last trap caught one, somehow, and it's right in the lab. Now maybe we can get somewhere getting rid of these nasty little—" He broke off, glancing anxiously over his shoulder. His voice lowered cautiously. "Now, look, Barney. Get down here right away, and don't—*please* don't—say anything to the papers. We'd be mobbed. Just get down there, and maybe we can squeeze something out of this one."

Barney flipped the switch, his heart thumping wildly, and struggled back into his topcoat. He almost collided with his wife as he started for the door.

"What's all the excitement?" she asked, her pretty face clouding. "And where do you think you're going in such a rush?"

Barney groped on the shelf for his hat. "We've caught a Vimp," he said. "I'm going back to the lab to look it over."

"Very funny," said Flora humorlessly, her gray eyes wide with displeasure. "Now tell me another. Vimp my eye. You'd be the last man in the world to catch a Vimp."

"This is the real thing, and no joke," Barney said. "Martin has a Vimp down at the lab, and I'm going to look at it. I'm sorry to leave you alone but—" He adjusted his hat and stepped resolutely out the door.

His car was parked in the driveway. He had almost reached it when he noticed the steering wheel sitting loose on the lawn, and saw the fuzzy bottom sticking out from under the hood. *"Hey!"* he screamed in a burst of rage, running to the car and shaking his fist in despair. "Get out of there! Scram! Beat it!"

The bottom disappeared abruptly, and a wrinkled brown face arose from the hood, blinking balefully. Barney ducked as a spark plug whistled past his ear, helpless rage rising in his throat as the little brown creature darted across the lawn and stopped near the hedge, hopping up and down, beating its hands together in malignant glee. Barney peered under the hood with a sinking feeling in the pit of his stomach. The distributor was gone, the spark plugs all broken off, the generator twisted, and three bolts completely unscrewed from the engine block.

Barney swore and shook his fist at the little brown fuzz-ball disappearing under the hedge. Slamming down the hood angrily, he strode down to the corner and hailed a passing cab. This, he reflected sourly, had all the makings of a very bad night.

The Vimps had first appeared, quite suddenly, one hot August afternoon about a year before, an appearance quite as remarkable as the creatures themselves. A certain farmer's small daughter had come into the house bawling that afternoon, a large red welt on her arm, babbling some sort of gibberish about "little monkeys coming out of the ground." Fabrication or not, her arm was visibly sore, so the farmer investigated. He found them, down in the south pasture, coming one by one from a strange, round, shimmering hole in the ground: small, fuzzy, gibbon-like, quick, popping rapidly up and out, and darting over to stand with the group already through, hissing and snarling at the farmer and each other. About two dozen of them emerged, and then the shiny ring vanished quite suddenly, and the little brown creatures started away, moving in sudden spurts of remarkable speed, fanning out to disappear into the woods. The farmer reported the occurrence to the local newspaper, and got himself laughed at. After all, little monkeys *don't* just pop out of the ground. And indeed, for almost a week nothing more was seen or heard of them. The farmer scratched his stubbled chin in puzzlement, thrashed his daughter soundly for telling such tales, and went back to plowing.

It took just about a week. First the neighboring town saw them, three of them trotting in an odd three-legged gait down the middle of Main Street, snarling and snapping at everyone in sight. Then reports began to come in: from the elderly maiden schoolteacher who saw a little fuzzy animal drawing improper pictures on the sidewalk with chalk as she passed by; from the business man who came out one morning to find his spanking new automobile completely dismantled on the lawn; from the minister who tried to shoo one of the little brown fuzz-balls off the rectory porch, and said many unministerial things when he got himself bitten for his pains. The original two dozen grew to four, and then to eight, as the little creatures multiplied impossibly and spread.

They got their name when an enterprising reporter quite accurately dubbed them Very Important Menacing Problems, and the wire services and broadcasters used the expected abbreviation, VIMPs. They reached the neighboring city in ever-growing numbers, biting people, ripping their clothes, screaming gibberish at them, raiding refrigerators, chewing putty out of window panes, breaking open mailboxes and switching letters, jamming motors, switching street-car tracks, hissing and snarling and spitting and glowering, jumping into people's hair and biting their ankles. Complaints rose in a wave, demands that someone, somehow, figure out how to get rid of these Vimps. After all, people said, rats could be exterminated, and mosquitoes, and Vimps were far more annoying than either.

But the Vimps presented a slightly more difficult problem. In the first place, nobody could catch them. They moved with incredible speed, so fast that they couldn't even be shot. And they were clever, so astonishingly clever! Traps were built, impossibly complicated traps, and the Vimps stole the bait from them, and hissed in derision when the people tried to figure out how the bait could be gotten *out* without a Vimp getting *in*. Complaints continued to billow throughout the ensuing months as the Vimps waxed and grew strong, tormenting people, pestering, annoying, biting, scratching. Within months there wasn't a community in the land, large or small, that hadn't seen one of the nasty little creatures, and still not one of them had been caught. Ships were plagued with them at sea, and angry reports began reaching the Capitol from India, Europe, and Asia. The towns and cities appealed to their states for aid, and the states begged the National Legislature to do something, *anything,* to get rid of this fuzzy brown plague that had invaded the land. People grew angry, and the angrier they grew, the more Vimps seemed to turn up to make them still angrier.

And then the Committee was set up—a slightly confused Committee, to be sure, since nobody really knew what sort of approach to use on the Vimps. Sociologists argued that they were intelligent creatures, worthy of careful sociological study. Physicists insisted that however they had arrived, by time-screen or matter transmitter, they had knowledge that could be of vast importance to the world of science. The physicians placidly agreed that if Vimps came from another world, and obviously they must have, they would soon die off from native diseases. The average man in the street grated his teeth, slapped a furry, snarling fuzz-ball off his neck, and troubled deaf Heaven with his seething prayer that *somebody* do *something* —at least catch one, or do *something*.

And the National Committee for Vimp Control finally managed to bring together such a curious admixture of viewpoints as Barney Holder, mild student and teacher of sociology, and Hugo Martin, stormy U.S. Navy consultant on rat extermination, and the Committee dropped the problem squarely, wholeheartedly, and none too comfortably into their laps.

The Vimp sat in the middle of the cage, glowering at them from button-black eyes, its round ears sticking straight out from its fuzzy round head, its little monkey face wrinkled. Two large incisors in the front of its mouth were flanked on either side by a double row of needle-sharp teeth, and it balanced itself nervously on its three scrawny legs. It looked for all the world like an angry little two-foot gnome, sitting back on its haunches, hating people.

"It doesn't look pleased," remarked Barney, turning his chair so he could see it more clearly.

Hugo Martin wiped his beefy face with a large handkerchief and chuckled unpleasantly. "You should have been here when it found it couldn't get loose," he growled. "I don't know if it has a language or not, but if it has it was using every dirty word it knows. Mad? You never saw anything so mad!" He licked his heavy lips with relish. "I'm thinking it's high time one of *them* got mad."

Barney grinned and watched the Vimp. "I still don't get it," he said finally. "These little beasties have licked every trap we've been able to cook up, yet this one was fairly obvious—a wide-open mirror maze with a weight-sensitive trapdoor." He looked up at the heavy man across the room from him. "How did it work?"

Martin scowled at the Vimp. "Got taken up with its own meanness, I'd say. It got in the building this noon, and spent the afternoon tormenting the laboratory cat. Made the cat so mad she could hardly see straight, and finally she ran into the maze to get away from it. Then she got caught, which made her madder yet, and the next thing I knew the Vimp was right in the trap with her, pulling her tail and yowling to beat Ned. The Vimp didn't seem to notice that it was trapped until we let Puss out the bait-hole! And then—" he grinned maliciously —"blooey! We had one mad little animal!"

Barney walked over to the cage, peered mildly in at the little brown gnome. The Vimp met him eye for eye, glowering malignantly. "Nice little Vimp," murmured Barney thoughtfully. The Vimp hunched its back and spat, never blinking its button-black eyes.

Barney extended his hand, his voice soft and soothing. "Come on, little fellow. Why not be friends? After all, now that you're here we might as well have a talk—OUCH!" He withdrew his hand sharply, saw the little semicircle of blood from the pinpoint teeth. The Vimp hopped up and down on one skinny leg, hissing and screeching in obvious delight. Barney felt his face flush angrily. "Now, now," he said unsteadily, "that wasn't nice." The Vimp sat back, scratched its white stomach, and glared.

Hugo Martin chuckled nastily. "You aren't going to get

anywhere with that approach," he said. "I got bit three times. Treat it mean, I say. Nasty little tyrant."

"No, no." Barney shook his head and ran a hand through his dark hair. "These little fellows are intelligent. They aren't stupid—why, up until now they've outsmarted every attempt to catch them. They *must* be able to think—and on a high order, too. And if they're intelligent, we've got to get through to them, somehow." He drew a pipe from his vest pocket and began stuffing the bowl. "If they *are* extraterrestrial life, they must have a remarkable knowledge of science to have gotten here at all. Maybe if we offered it some food—"

Martin wiped his forehead and snorted. "You may try, if you like," he growled. "I don't want to get close to it."

Barney took a small chunk of bread from the desk and advanced it to the cage, watching the fuzzy captive closely. The Vimp looked at the bread skeptically, his leg muscles tightening. Then with an incredibly swift motion he snatched the bread from Barney's fingers, leaving another welt on the back of his hand.

"Why, you dirty—" Barney slapped at the Vimp through the bars in quick rage. The Vimp crowded up close to the bars like a small vicious gibbon, black eyes gleaming malignantly, hissing, making nasty little sounds in its throat. Barney felt his face grow red as the creature hopped up and down on one foot, devouring the bread and making little noises of malicious delight.

Barney's hand shook, and he gripped the chair arm tightly as he sat down. "Very soon," he muttered, nursing his bitten hand, "I shall lose my temper." He looked up at Martin helplessly. "How could anything be so mean? What do you have to do to get a pleasant reaction from it?"

"Nothing will get a pleasant reaction from it," Martin retorted angrily. "These things haven't got any niceness in them."

"But there must be *some* way of reaching them, somehow." Barney rubbed his chin thoughtfully. "Look here," he said suddenly. "We've been getting all sorts of letters from people. The Vimps pester me and they pester you—but some people just *aren't bothered* by them."

Hugo Martin blinked incredulously. "I thought everybody was bothered by them."

Barney eyed the Vimp thoughtfully for a moment, then dug into his desk. "Not everyone," he said. "Here's a letter that came in from Translations Bureau yesterday." He drew out a large roll of parchment with a slip of office paper stapled to it.

"Translations Bureau?"

"Yes. It was from some place in India. Let's see now, it says:

" 'To our brethren of the West. We would remind you that all matter is nothing, only the spirit prevails. All bodies are of matter, bodies from this and all other worlds that are in God. He who has learned to ignore matter has put his first steps on the path of understanding. These you call Vimps, they too are but matter and as such can, in the proper time, be ignored and so rendered harmless.' "

Barney stopped.

"Yes, yes," exclaimed Hugo Martin, his pudgy face flushed excitedly. "How do they say to get rid of them?"

Barney let the letter drop to the floor. "They don't," he growled. "That's all they say. But hang it, there were other letters! Like the one from the Franciscan monk who advised that prayer and fasting would keep them away. Or the newlywed couple who said the Vimps wouldn't go near the church when they were being married, but invaded their cottage by the dozens on the fourth day of their honeymoon." Barney scratched his head, pondering.

"Religion!" yelped Martin, bouncing out of his chair. His cheeks puffed excitedly. "That ties it all in! Maybe they're afraid of it, or maybe they can't stand being prayed against. Maybe all we'd have to do to drive them away is to get Religion!" Martin walked about excitedly. "Maybe the sign of the Cross would keep the nasty things away."

Barney blinked. "Maybe there *is* a religious angle, at that," he said, suddenly excited. He stared hard at the Vimp, which was pouting angrily in a corner of the cage. "Let's go down and get some coffee and think this over."

They sat in the small coffee shop, Hugo Martin muttering to himself occasionally, Barney just sipping his coffee and thinking. Across the street a crowd had gathered in a little park, and a speaker had risen on a crude platform. Suddenly a loudspeaker blared in Barney's ear, jolting his mind away from Vimps.

"—it's the curse of the Devil coming to punish us sinful men," the voice was bellowing to the crowd, "and we've got to fight it, that's what we've got to do! We got to fight the Devil on his own ground! We got to get down on our knees and pray!"

The crowd inched closer, drinking in the fiery words. "He's brought the plague upon us for our sins!" the evangelist cried angrily. "We got to stand up and fight the Devil, we can't give in, 'cause when we give in the fires o' Hell will burn us, the sulfur and brimstone o' Hell will get at our very innards!" The rich hoarse voice roared across the street. "If we want to free ourselves, we got to get down on our knees and *pray!*" He scowled fiercely and shook his fist. "We got to cleanse ourselves 'fore the Lord Almighty will spare us."

Barney Holder was across the room in a minute, staring out the window at the gesticulating preacher. *"Look at that!"* he said.

"Yeah, that's just Preacher Simes. He gets up there and harangues every night, 'til he gets too violent."

"But look at the platform!"

The preacher was shouting louder, his face red with angry indignation. And up on the rostrum, staring at him with beady eyes, drinking in his every word, snarling at him, were five large, fuzzy Vimps.

"It's the curse of the Almighty visited on us!" The preacher paused to slap away a Vimp that had run up and bit him on the ear. "Get out of here, you damned little—I say, we got to *pray*!"

Suddenly the platform was alive with them, tearing at the preacher's trousers, unlacing his shoes, scrapping and scratching, hissing and yowling until the preacher, with a howl of anguished rage jumped from the platform like a crazy man and dashed, slapping and kicking, for the street.

Barney sank wearily into his chair. "Well," he said sadly, "there goes the Religion angle."

The captive Vimp started screeching and caterwauling as soon as they came into the lab, gnawing viciously at the bars, glaring at them with beady black eyes. "What are we going to do?" moaned Barney. "There must be some way to make them be nice."

"There's nothing we can do, I tell you." Hugo Martin scowled at the animal in the cage. "What we've got to do is find some way to kill them, that's all. We can't shoot them—they just dodge the bullets. They won't go near poison. And gas doesn't seem to bother them a bit." The big man kicked angrily at the cage. "I tell you, Barney, there's no use trying to contact them. They don't want to be friends. They're nasty clear through. And I've taken about all the plaguing from these little pests that I can stand. So has everyone else. They're driving people to their wits' end, and it's our job to find how to get rid of them." His voice lowered bitterly as he stared at Barney. "Three cars I've had to buy—three brand-new cars—because these things tear them apart. I'm being starved out of house and home because I can't buy food fast enough. I've got a whole tribe of them, living in my house, biting my children, laughing at me, scaring my wife, ripping out my plumbing. I can't take much more, I tell you. And all you can think of is contacting them! Bah! Find out how to kill them, I say."

The Vimp had shifted its attention to Martin, crowding close to the bars, watching the big man avidly, almost hungrily, as his voice rose to fever pitch. Barney watched the Vimp and felt a chill run up his spine. "Hugo," he said softly, "that little fellow is sensitive to you. Look at him! I'd swear he's drinking in every word you're saying."

"Well, I hope they choke him!" Martin roared, "because he's not coming out of that cage alive." He turned on the Vimp, glaring helplessly. "Pest! Why don't you go back where you came from?"

The telephone began blinking suddenly. Martin threw the Vimp a final bitter look and lifted the receiver. "Lab," he said. Then he grimaced and crooked a finger at Barney. "Just a minute, Flora—"

Barney took the receiver. "Yes, Flora," he said mildly. There was a long pause as the receiver squealed angrily. Finally: "Flora, I *told* you I was going to the lab. I may be here all night. Oh, you have, have you? Well, what am I supposed to do about it? Chase it out! I'm playing patty-cake with one down here." He slammed down the receiver, cutting off the angry chirping. "Something is going to have to be done," he muttered, as he stalked across the room, a harried look in his eyes. "Those Vimps have got Flora so worked up she won't give me a minute's rest."

Martin glanced up at him shrewdly. "Rumor has it that you and Flora were at it long before the Vimps came."

Barney shot him a black look, and shuffled back to the cage. "I can't even get along with my wife," he said miserably. "How can I make friends with one of these nasty little things?" He glared at the Vimp and the Vimp glared back at him with unabated fury. "Maybe we *should* just get rid of them." He turned to the fuzzy little animal furiously. "We could kill you, you know. We could starve you to death, or we could bring in a machine gun, a *fast* machine gun, and riddle you. We're just trying to be nice, but we can wipe you out clean if you don't co-operate."

The Vimp sat straight up, just as though it had understood, and spat on the floor with magnificent disdain. Then it turned around and walked to a corner and sat down on its three legs, blinking owlishly. Barney sat watching it for a long time.

He was home early for supper the next evening. Flora met him at the door, a bedraggled combination of tears, anger, and fright. "Those *nasty* little things got in the house again," she wailed. "I couldn't help letting them in, and one of them bit me." She turned on Barney bitterly. "What kind of man are you, Barney Holder? You were supposed to be so smart, such a clever man, and you can't even find a way to keep them out of your own house. You don't care what happens to me when you're gone. I thought I married a pretty smart fellow, and he turns out to be a second-rate teacher that can't even outwit a

—a Vimp!" She burst into tears, and sank down on the sofa, nursing her bitten ankle.

"That's not fair," snapped Barney, "and you know it! I'm doing the best I can."

"Well, your best just isn't good enough. *Look! They're right here in the living room watching us!*"

They were, all right. Two fuzzy brown animals were sitting there, their upper lips curled, snarling at each other with bared teeth, watching Barney and Flora out of the corner of their evil little eyes. They slapped one another and pulled each other's fur, biting and spitting at each other. The larger one threw a haymaker that spun the smaller head over heels across the room with a venomous snarl, but it picked itself up and came back, screeching all the louder, to clout the large one in the face with a small doubled fist. The battle raged, but there was something peculiar about their fighting, Barney thought. A very curious fight. They snarled, and bit, and pounded, and screeched, but somehow—

"Flora!" Sudden light burst in Barney's brain, an idea, incredible, ridiculous. He looked wonderingly at his wife, and then back at the snarling fuzz-balls. "Flora! They aren't fighting! They're making love!"

Flora blinked through tearful eyes, looking at the Vimps in alarm. The small one raked its claws across the other's face. "Garbage," said Flora succinctly.

"No, no—look at them!" Barney's eyes were suddenly very bright, and in an instant he was across the room, standing over his wife. "Stand up," he commanded.

Flora blinked twice. "I will not!"

Barney swiftly reached down, grabbed her wrist, and jerked her to her feet. Before she could move he took her fiercely in his arms, and planted his lips hard on hers. She squeaked through the kiss, twisting to push him away. "Barney, stop it!"

"Shut up!"

Some urgency in his voice stopped her, almost frightened her. "You will sit down," Barney whispered excitedly. "Then you will kiss me, right here on the couch. And you will kindly shut up while you're doing it!"

She sat down, bewildered, and Barney sat down beside her, tightened his arms about her again.

"Barney—"

The room was silent for a long moment.

Then a longer moment.

"Barney." Her voice was softer now, her face softer, sweeter than Barney had seen it in a long time. He kissed her again, the Vimps forgotten. "Barney—it's been a long time since we've kissed on the davenport."

"Ummmmmmmmm."

"An *awful* long time."

"Too long, Flora."

"We should—maybe try it more often—"

A sound, an odd sound. Almost as if by signal they looked up. They saw the Vimps, angry eyes staring at them—the two Vimps that had forgotten their fighting, and were backing away from them, backs hunched, hissing, spitting, *trembling*.

Quite suddenly the Vimps turned and bolted for the door.

"You," said Hugo Martin unhappily, "have gone off your trolley. You don't know what you're saying. You're crazy. And if you think I'm going to swallow that sort of—of nonsense—" he swallowed, his double chin bobbing—"you're double-crazy," He lumbered back to his desk, his red face glowing.

Barney smiled easily. His lean jaw was clean-shaven, his

eyes bright. "I'm not wrong, Hugo. I've got the answer. It may sound ridiculous, but the whole business is ridiculous. And it'll work, I'll stake my salary on it!"

He sat down in the chair opposite the Vimp cage, easing his sore arm. "Look at it this way," he said. "Wherever men have gone, into new places, new countries, what have they done? Have they adapted themselves to their new environment? Have they tried to 'go native,' to actually *be* like the people they found? Have they tried to fall into native economic patterns, culture patterns? They have not. China, Africa, India—wherever they've gone, it's been the same old story. They've tried to change the environment to suit themselves. They've tried to make it like the one back home. The temperature, the habits, the *culture*. The last thing men would dream of would be to alter their culture patterns to match an alien environment. And if they found things, where they were, to be unchangeable, hostile, inalterably foreign, they've always, always turned around and come home."

"But the Vimps!" Martin said impatiently. "I don't see what this has to do with—"

"Everything," said Barney flatly. "The Vimps are from another planet, another world, somewhere. They're intelligent, all right, and they have a culture, too—a rather nasty culture, it seems. With men, the *basic* culture is founded on peace and familial love—the ancient sign of the raised right hand, saying, 'I have no weapons.' Basically, man seeks to live in peace undisturbed, and takes that peace with him to alien lands, and where those lands are too hostile, too unpeaceful, he has ultimately come home, beaten.

"Still, another world—a Vimp world—might have a culture on a different basis. A basis impossible for men to tolerate. Not based on peace at all, you see. Based on hate. Pure, rich, ripe, unadulterated hate."

Martin's eyes widened. "You mean—"

"I mean they hate each other and everything else. Hate is their life force, the foundation of their moral values. They live, eat, sleep, and die with hate in their every thought. The idea of kindness and love is foreign to them, unbelievable, frightening, alien. They came here without the barest inkling of the abstract concept of love, and they expected to find hate here, too. And what they found was fearful to them, hateful, hostile—a culture based on love and peace. But they saw, or somehow felt, that men were capable, under certain circumstances, of hatefulness, and that was all the Vimps needed. They just had to change things a little, was all. All they wanted was to be hated!"

"Well, they're getting what they want!" snarled Hugo Martin. "I hate them, I hope to tell you. Lord! How I hate them. I hate them so much—"

"And you seem to draw them, don't you? You have them all over your house, you hate them so much. They don't want anything to do with mystics, or monks—they torment cats and dogs within an inch of their lives, but they'd never, never bother a cow. They come to you because you provide just the hate-filled environment they *have to have*. Don't you see the implications, man? If you hate them, they'll stay around. Multiply. Thrive." He looked up at the large man slyly. "But if you *love* them—"

Hugo Martin's heavy jaw quivered, and something akin to tears appeared in his stricken eyes. "Barney," he choked weakly, "now, wait a minute, Barney, you *can't* be right." He glanced fearfully at the Vimp glaring at him through the bars. "Anything but that, Barney—I—I couldn't *make* myself—"

"You'll just *have* to love them," said Barney firmly.

Tears of frustration rolled down Martin's fat cheeks. He started toward the cage, dragging his feet like a child, then stopped. "But—but what can I *do*?" he wailed. "It's like loving a centipede, or something. It's—it's sacrilegious." He extended a hand, tentatively, toward the bars, drew it back with a jerk when the Vimp snarled. "Oh, Barney, I *can't!*"

"Look," said Barney, grinning. "I'll show you." He pulled on a pair of heavy leather gloves. Then he walked over to the cage, where the Vimp was eyeing him angrily. Barney extended a chunk of bread through the bars. "Come on, Vimp. Nice little Vimp." His voice was soft and soothing.

The Vimp snatched the bread and bit him viciously on the hand. Barney felt the anger rise, but he grinned tightly and reached in to pet the creature on the head. "Sweet little Vimp," he cooed. "*Nice* little Vimp."

The Vimp bit him again, harder. Then it backed away, hissing, a baffled look in its eyes. It began snarling, making hateful noises in the back of its throat, baring its teeth.

"Such a cute little fellow, too," said Barney, gritting his teeth. "We're going to be such *good* friends! Come on, little fellow, let me pet you."

The Vimp was thoroughly alarmed now, hunching its back, spitting, pressing back against the cage. Its little black eyes blazed with fear as it struggled to push backward through the bars.

"Let him go," said Barney softly. "Open the trap and let him out."

Martin clenched his big fist, walking slowly to the trap. "Gently," said Barney. "Whatever you do, *don't lose your temper*."

Martin opened the trap gingerly. "Nice little Vimp," he rumbled tearfully. "Come on out, you dirty little—"

Barney coughed gently. Then he said, "Go on home, now,

little fellow. Run along and tell your friends how pleasant and happy things are going to be from now on."

The Vimp hissed and snarled, and suddenly bolted, a thousand devils at his heels. Through the window he went, pausing only to hurl back one hair-curling Vimp invective as he disappeared over the sill.

Barney heaved a deep sigh, and grinned at Hugo Martin. "There," he said.

"It won't work," wailed Martin. "We never should have let it go. It'll just be back to torment us again."

"Not if we *love* it, it won't." Barney grinned happily. "All it takes to drive it away is a peaceful, pleasant, serene atmosphere. That's hard to manage, with Vimps around—but people have got to manage it. It's the only way."

Hugo Martin looked at him entreatingly. "You don't know what you're asking for, Barney. Peaceful, serene atmosphere —people couldn't manage that even before the Vimps came. And *nobody* can be nice to a Vimp. People just won't do it."

"Oh, yes they will," said Barney softly, "if they want to get rid of them badly enough."

The word went out on the radios that afternoon, hit the evening papers, and exploded throughout the country. The incredible word, the ridiculous word—and people stopped swearing at Vimps to listen, and laugh derisively, and went back to swearing at Vimps. And a few enterprising individuals tried it, and found, miraculously, that it worked. One by one the Vimps began leaving, snarling, bolting like three-legged lightning out of house after house. The news spread fast; people stopped their work, their bickering and fighting, and slapping of Vimps, and saw, wonderingly, how well it worked.

Over town and country and village they tried it, and it worked, like a balm over the land.

Finally one afternoon the radio reported that a silvery ring had appeared in a farmer's south pasture, and that Vimps by the pack and drove, hundreds and thousands of Vimps were trooping down. Barney and Flora Holder were there, along with the crowd, a curious crowd, filled with curious emotions, not knowing for sure exactly *how* they felt. But they were loving Vimps with all the compassionate love they could muster. For very dear life they were loving the Vimps.

Flora snuggled closer to Barney and smiled happily up at him. "It's been almost fun watching them go."

Barney grinned. "It *has* been a tranquil couple of weeks," he admitted.

Flora looked up at him, her eyes moist, the coldness and anger gone from her face. "I'm—I know it sounds silly, but I'm almost sorry to see them go. We—Barney, can't we pretend there are still a couple around?"

The dwindling crowd of fuzzy brown creatures disappeared one by one down the silvery ring, hunching their backs at the crowd, curling their upper lips and baring their teeth in angry snarls, hissing, scurrying, pulling each other's hair, screeching. Finally the last one stood on the edge of the ring, spat eloquently and malignantly on the ground before him, and hopped in. The ring shimmered, wavered, and vanished.

As though waking from an enchanted spell, the crowd released a long sigh, and the people looked about, seeing each other for the first time, an aura of puzzled contentment rising like a wave. Barney started up the ridge toward the car, Flora's hand tight in his. He smiled down at her, met her happy eyes. "I don't know about the other people," he said softly. "But as far as I'm concerned, the Vimps never left."

Letter of the Law

THE place was dark and damp, and smelled like moldy leaves. Meyerhoff followed the huge, bear-like Altairian guard down the slippery flagstones of the corridor, sniffing the dead, musty air with distaste. He drew his carefully tailored Terran styled jacket closer about his shoulders, shivering as his eyes avoided the black, yawning cell-holes they were passing. His foot slipped on the slimy flags from time to time, and finally he paused to wipe the caked mud from his trouser leg. "How much farther is it?" he shouted angrily.

The guard waved a heavy paw vaguely into the blackness ahead. Quite suddenly the corridor took a sharp bend, and the Altairian stopped, producing a huge key ring from some obscure fold of his hairy hide. "I still don't see any reason for all the fuss," he grumbled in a wounded tone. "We've treated him like a brother."

One of the huge steel doors clicked open. Meyerhoff peered

into the blackness, catching a vaguely human outline against the back wall. "Harry?" he called sharply.

There was a startled gasp from within, and a skinny, gnarled little man suddenly appeared in the guard's light, like a grotesque, twisted ghost out of the blackness. Wide blue eyes regarded Meyerhoff from beneath uneven black eyebrows, and then the little man's face broke into a crafty grin. "Paul! So they sent *you!* I knew I could count on it!" He executed a deep, awkward bow, motioning Meyerhoff into the dark cubicle. "Not much to offer you," he said slyly, "but it's the best I can do under the circumstances."

Meyerhoff scowled, and turned abruptly to the guard. "We'll have some privacy now, if you please. Interplanetary ruling. And leave us the light."

The guard grumbled, and started for the door. "It's about time you showed up!" cried the little man in the cell. "Great day! Lucky they sent you, pal. Why, I've been in here for years—"

"Look, Zeckler, the name is Meyerhoff, and I'm not your pal," Meyerhoff snapped. "And you've been here for two weeks, three days, and approximately four hours. You're getting as bad as your gentle guards when it comes to bandying the truth around." He peered through the dim light at the gaunt face of the prisoner. Zeckler's face was dark with a week's beard, and his bloodshot eyes belied the cocky grin on his lips. His clothes were smeared and sodden, streaked with great splotches of mud and moss. Meyerhoff's face softened a little. "So Harry Zeckler's in a jam again," he said. "You *look* as if they'd treated you like a brother."

The little man snorted. "These overgrown teddy-bears don't know what brotherhood means, nor humanity, either. Bread and water I've been getting, nothing more, and then only if they feel like bringing it down." He sank wearily down on the rock bench along the wall. "I thought you'd never get here! I sent an appeal to the Terran Consulate the first day I was arrested. What happened? I mean, all they had to do was get a man over here, get the extradition papers signed, and provide transportation off the planet for me. Why so much time? I've been sitting here rotting—" He broke off in mid-sentence and stared at Meyerhoff. "You *brought* the papers, didn't you? I mean, we can leave now?"

Meyerhoff stared at the little man with a mixture of pity and disgust. "You are a prize fool," he said finally. "Did you know that?"

Zeckler's eyes widened. "What do you mean, fool? So I spend a couple of weeks in this pneumonia trap. The deal was worth it! I've got three million credits sitting in the Terran Consulate on Altair V, just waiting for me to walk in and pick them up. Three million credits—do you hear? That's enough to set me up for life!"

Meyerhoff nodded grimly. "*If* you live long enough to walk in and pick them up, that is."

"What do you mean, if?"

Meyerhoff sank down beside the man, his voice a tense whisper in the musty cell. "I mean that right now you are practically dead. You may not know it, but you are. You walk into a newly opened planet with your smart little bag of tricks, walk in here with a shaky passport and no permit, with no knowledge of the natives outside of two paragraphs of inaccuracies in the Explorer's Guide, and even then you're not content to come in and sell something legitimate, something the natives might conceivably be able to use. No, nothing so simple for you. You have to pull your usual high-pressure stuff. And this time, buddy, you're paying the piper."

"You mean I'm not being extradited?"

Meyerhoff grinned unpleasantly. "I mean precisely that. You've committed a crime here—a major crime. The Altairians are sore about it. And the Terran Consulate isn't willing to sell all the trading possibilities here down the river just to get you out of a mess. You're going to stand trial—and these natives are out to get you. Personally, I think they're *going* to get you."

Zeckler stood up shakily. "You can't believe anything the natives say," he said uneasily. "They're pathological liars. Why, you should see what they tried to sell *me*! You've never seen such a pack of liars as these critters." He glanced up at Meyerhoff. "They'll probably drop a little fine on me and let me go."

"A little fine of one Terran neck." Meyerhoff grinned nastily. "You've committed the most heinous crime these creatures can imagine, and they're going to get you for it if it's the last thing they do. I'm afraid, my friend, that your con-man days are over."

Zeckler fished in the other man's pocket, extracted a cigarette, and lighted it with trembling fingers. "It's bad, then," he said finally.

"It's bad, all right."

Some shadow of the sly, elfin grin crept over the little con-man's face. "Well, at any rate, I'm glad they sent you over," he said weakly. "Nothing like a good lawyer to handle a trial."

"*Lawyer*? Not me! Oh, no. Sorry, but no thanks." Meyerhoff chuckled. "I'm your advisor, old boy. Nothing else. I'm here to keep you from botching things up still worse for the Trading Commission, that's all. I wouldn't get tangled up in a mess with those creatures for anything!" He shook his head. "You're your own lawyer, Mr. Super-salesman. It's all your show. And you'd better get your head out of the sand, or you're going to lose a case like it's never been lost before!"

Meyerhoff watched the man's pale face, and shook his head. In a way, he thought, it was a pity to see such a change in the rosy-cheeked, dapper, cocksure little man who had talked his way glibly in and out of more jams than Meyerhoff could count. Trading brought scalpers; it was almost inevitable that where rich and unexploited trading ground was uncovered, it would first fall prey to the fast-trading boys. They spread out from Terra with the first wave of exploration—the slick, fast-talking con-men who could work new territories unfettered by the legal restrictions that soon closed down the more established planets. The first men in were the richest out, and through some curious quirk of the Terrestrial mind, they knew they could count on Terran protection, however crooked and underhand their methods.

But occasionally a situation arose where the civilization and social practices of the alien victims made it unwise to tamper with them. Altair I had been recognized at once by the Trading Commission as a commercial prize of tremendous value, but early reports had warned of the danger of wildcat trading on the little, musty, jungle-like planet with its shaggy, three-eyed inhabitants—warned specifically against the confidence tactics so frequently used—but there was always somebody, Meyerhoff reflected sourly, who just didn't get the word.

Zeckler puffed nervously on his cigarette, his narrow face a study in troubled concentration. "But I didn't *do* anything!" he exploded finally. "So I pulled an old con game. So what? Why should they get so excited? So I clipped a few thousand credits, pulled a little fast business." He shrugged eloquently, spreading his hands. "Everybody's doing it. They do it to each other without batting an eye. You should *see* these critters operate on each other. Why, my little scheme was peanuts by comparison."

Meyerhoff pulled a pipe from his pocket, and began stuffing the bowl with infinite patience. "And precisely what sort of con game was it?" he asked quietly.

Zeckler shrugged again. "The simplest, tiredest, moldiest old racket that ever made a quick nickel. Remember the old Terran gag about the Brooklyn Bridge? The same thing. Only these critters didn't want bridges. They wanted land—this gooey, slimy swamp they call 'farm land.' So I gave them what they wanted. I just sold them some land."

Meyerhoff nodded fiercely. "You sure did. A hundred square kilos at a swipe. Only you sold the same hundred square kilos to a dozen different natives." Suddenly he threw back his hands and roared. "Of all the things you *shouldn't* have done—"

"But what's a chunk of land?"

Meyerhoff shook his head hopelessly. "If you hadn't been so greedy, you'd have found out what a chunk of land was to these natives before you started peddling it. You'd have found out other things about them, too. You'd have learned that in spite of all their bumbling and fussing and squabbling they're not so dull. You'd have found out that they're marsupials, and that two out of five of them get thrown out of their mother's pouch before they're old enough to survive. You'd have realized that they have to start fighting for individual rights almost as soon as they're born. Anything goes, as long as it benefits them as individuals."

Meyerhoff grinned at the little man's horrified face. "Never heard of that, had you? And you've never heard of other things, too. You've probably never heard that there are just too many Altairians here for the food their planet can supply, and their diet is so finicky that they just can't live on anything that doesn't grow here. And consequently, land is the key factor in their economy, not money; nothing but land. To get land, it's every man for himself, and the loser starves, and their entire legal and monetary system revolves on that principle. They've built up the most confusing and impossible system of barter and trade imaginable, aimed at individual survival, with land as the value behind the credit. That explains the lying—of course they're liars, with an economy like that. They've completely missed the concept of truth. Pathological? You bet they're pathological! Only a fool would tell the truth when his life depended on his being a better liar than the next guy! Lying is the time-honored tradition, with their entire legal system built around it."

Zeckler snorted. "But how could they *possibly* have a legal system? I mean, if they don't recognize the truth when it slaps them in the face?"

Meyerhoff shrugged. "As we understand legal systems, I suppose they don't have one. They have only the haziest idea what truth represents, and they've shrugged off the idea as impossible and useless." He chuckled maliciously. "So you went out and found a chunk of ground in the uplands, and sold it to a dozen separate, self-centered, half-starved natives! Encroachment on private property is legal grounds for murder on this planet, and twelve of them descended on the same chunk of land at the same time, all armed with title-deeds." Meyerhoff sighed. "You've got twelve mad Altairians in your hair. You've got a mad planet in your hair. And in the meantime, Terra's most valuable uranium source in five centuries is threatening to cut off supply unless they see your blood splattered liberally all the way from here to the equator."

Zeckler was visibly shaken. "Look," he said weakly, "so I

wasn't so smart. What am I going to do? I mean, are you going to sit quietly by and let them butcher me? How could I defend myself in a legal setup like *this*?"

Meyerhoff smiled coolly. "You're going to get your sly little con-man brain to working, I think," he said softly. "By Interplanetary Rules, they have to give you a trial in Terran legal form—judge, jury, court procedure, all that folderol. They think it's a big joke—after all, what could a judicial oath mean to them?—but they agreed. Only thing is, they're going to hang you, if they die trying. So you'd better get those stunted little wits of yours clicking—and if you try to implicate *me*, even a little bit, I'll be out of there so fast you won't know what happened."

With that Meyerhoff walked to the door. He jerked it inward sharply, and spilled two guards over on their faces. "Privacy," he grunted, and started back up the slippery corridor.

It certainly *looked* like a courtroom, at any rate. In the front of the long, damp stone room was a bench, with a seat behind it, and a small straight chair to the right. To the left was a stand with twelve chairs—larger chairs, with a railing running along the front. The rest of the room was filled almost to the door with seats facing the bench. Zeckler followed the shaggy-haired guard into the room, nodding approvingly. "Not such a bad arrangement," he said. "They must have gotten the idea fast."

Meyerhoff wiped the perspiration from his forehead, and shot the little con-man a stony glance. "At least you've got a courtroom, a judge, and a jury for this mess. Beyond that—" He shrugged eloquently. "I can't make any promises."

In the back of the room a door burst open with a bang. Loud, harsh voices were heard as half a dozen of the huge

Altairians attempted to push through the door at once. Zeckler clamped on the headset to his translator unit, and watched the hubbub in the anteroom with growing alarm. Finally the question of precedent seemed to be settled, and a group of the Altairians filed in, in order of stature, stalking across the room in flowing black robes, pug-nosed faces glowering with self-importance. They descended upon the jury box, grunting and scrapping with each other for the first-row seats, and the judge took his place with obvious satisfaction behind the heavy wooden bench. Finally, the prosecuting attorney appeared, flanked by two clerks, who took their places beside him. The prosecutor eyed Zeckler with cold malevolence, then turned and delivered a sly wink at the judge.

In a moment the room was a hubbub as it filled with the huge, bumbling, bear-like creatures, jostling each other and fighting for seats, growling and complaining. Two small fights broke out in the rear, but were quickly subdued by the group of gendarmes guarding the entrance. Finally the judge glared down at Zeckler with all three eyes, and pounded the bench top with a wooden mallet until the roar of activity subsided. The jurymen wriggled uncomfortably in their seats, exchanging winks, and finally turned their attention to the front of the court.

"We are reading the case of the people of Altair I," the judge's voice roared out, "against one Harry Zeckler—" he paused for a long, impressive moment—"Terran." The courtroom immediately burst into an angry growl, until the judge pounded the bench five or six times more. "This—creature—is hereby accused of the following crimes," the judge bellowed. "Conspiracy to overthrow the government of Altair I. Brutal murder of seventeen law-abiding citizens of the village of Karzan at the third hour before dawn in the second period after his arrival. Desecration of the Temple of our beloved Goddess Zermat, Queen of the Harvest. Conspiracy with the lesser gods to cause the unprecedented drought in the Dermatti section of our fair globe. Obscene exposure of his pouch-marks in a public square. Four separate and distinct charges of jail-break and bribery—" The judge pounded the bench for order —"Espionage with the accursed scum of Altair II in preparation for Interplanetary invasion."

The little con-man's jaw sagged lower and lower, the color draining from his face. He turned, wide-eyed, to Meyerhoff, then back to the judge.

"The Chairman of the Jury," said the Judge succinctly, "will read the verdict."

The little native in the front of the jury-box popped up like a puppet on a string. "Defendant found guilty on all counts," he said.

"Defendant is guilty! The court will pronounce sentence—"

"Now wait a minute!" Zeckler was on his feet, wild-eyed. "What kind of railroad job—"

The judge blinked disappointedly at Paul Meyerhoff. "Not yet?" he asked, unhappily.

"No." Meyerhoff's hands twitched nervously. "Not yet, Your Honor. Later, Your Honor. The trial comes *first.*"

The judge looked as if his candy had been stolen. "But you *said* I should call for the verdict."

"Later. You have to have the trial before you can have the verdict."

The Altairian shrugged indifferently. "Now—later—" he muttered.

"Have the prosecutor call his first witness," said Meyerhoff.

Zeckler leaned over, his face ashen. "These charges," he whispered. "They're insane!"

"Of course they are," Meyerhoff whispered back.

"But what am I going to—"

"Sit tight. Let *them* set things up."

"But those *lies*. They're liars, the whole pack of them—" He broke off as the prosecutor roared a name.

The shaggy brute who took the stand was wearing a bright purple hat which sat rakishly over one ear. He grinned the Altairian equivalent of a hungry grin at the prosecutor. Then he cleared his throat and started. "This Terran riffraff—"

"The oath," muttered the judge. "We've got to have the oath."

The prosecutor nodded, and four natives moved forward, carrying huge inscribed marble slabs to the front of the court. One by one the chunks were reverently piled in a heap at the witness's feet. The witness placed a huge, hairy paw on the cairn, and the prosecutor said, "Do you swear to tell the truth, the whole truth, and nothing but the truth, so help you—" he paused to squint at the paper in his hand, and finished on a puzzled note, "—Goddess?"

The witness removed the paw from the rock pile long enough to scratch his ear. Then he replaced it, and replied, "Of course," in an injured tone.

"Then tell this court what you have seen of the activities of this abominable wretch."

The witness settled back into the chair, fixing one eye on Zeckler's face, another on the prosecutor, and closing the third as if in meditation. "I think it happened on the fourth night of the seventh crossing of Altair II (may the Goddess cast a drought upon it)—or was it the seventh night of the fourth crossing?—" he grinned apologetically at the judge—"when I was making my way back through town toward my blessed land-plot, minding my own business, Your Honor, after weeks of bargaining for the crop I was harvesting. Suddenly from the shadow of the building, this creature—" he waved a paw at Zeckler—"stopped me in my tracks with a vicious cry. He had a weapon I'd never seen before, and before I could find my voice he forced me back against the wall. I could see by the cruel glint in his eyes that there was no warmth, no sympathy in his heart, that I was—"

"Objection!" Zeckler squealed plaintively, jumping to his feet. "This witness can't even remember what night he's talking about!"

The judge looked startled. Then he pawed feverishly through his bundle of notes. "Overruled," he said abruptly. "Continue, please."

The witness glowered at Zeckler. "As I was saying before this loutish interruption," he muttered, "I could see that I was face to face with the most desperate of criminal types, even for Terrans. Note the shape of his head, the flabbiness of his ears. I was petrified with fear. And then, helpless as I was, this two-legged abomination began to shower me with threats of evil to my blessed home, dark threats of poisoning my land unless I would tell him where he could find the resting place of our blessed Goddess—"

"I never saw him before in my life," Zeckler moaned to Meyerhoff. "Listen to him! Why should I care where their Goddess—"

Meyerhoff gave him a stony look. "The Goddess runs things around here. She makes it rain. If it doesn't rain, somebody's insulted her. It's very simple."

"But how can I fight testimony like that?"

"I doubt if you *can* fight it."

"But they can't prove a word of it—" He looked at the jury, who were listening enraptured to the second witness on the stand. This one was testifying regarding the butcherous slaughter of eighteen (or was it twenty-three? Oh, yes, twenty-three) women and children in the suburban village of Karzan. The pogrom, it seemed, had been accomplished by an energy weapon which ate great, gaping holes in the sides of buildings. A third witness took the stand, continuing the drone as the room grew hotter and muggier. Zeckler grew paler and paler, his eyes turning glassy as the testimony piled up. "But it's not *true*," he whispered to Meyerhoff.

"Of course it isn't! Can't you understand? *These people have no regard for truth.* It's stupid, to them, silly, a mark of low intelligence. The only thing in the world they have any respect for is a liar bigger and more skillful than they are."

Zeckler jerked around abruptly as he heard his name bellowed out. "Does the defendant have anything to say before the jury delivers the verdict?"

"Do I have—" Zeckler was across the room in a flash, his pale cheeks suddenly taking on a feverish glow. He sat down gingerly on the witness chair, facing the judge, his eyes bright with fear and excitement. "Your—Your Honor, I—I have a statement to make which will have a most important bearing on this case. You must listen with the greatest care." He glanced quickly at Meyerhoff, and back to the judge. "Your Honor," he said in a hushed voice. "You are in gravest of danger. All of you. Your lives—your very land is at stake."

The judge blinked, and shuffled through his notes hurriedly as a murmur arose in the court. "Our land?"

"Your lives, your land, everything you hold dear," Zeckler said quickly, licking his lips nervously. "You must try to understand me—" he glanced apprehensively over his shoulder —"now, because I may not live long enough to repeat what I am about to tell you—"

The murmur quieted down, all ears straining in their headsets to hear his words. "These charges," he continued, "all of them—they're perfectly true. At least, they *seem* to be perfectly true. But in every instance, I was working with heart and soul, risking my life, for the welfare of your beautiful planet."

There was a loud hiss from the back of the court. Zeckler frowned and rubbed his hands together. "It was my misfortune," he said, "to go to the wrong planet when I first came to Altair from my homeland on Terra. I—I landed on Altair II, a grave mistake, but as it turned out, a very fortunate error. Because in attempting to arrange trading in that frightful place, I made certain contacts." His voice trembled, and sank lower. "I learned the horrible thing which is about to happen to this planet, at the hands of those barbarians. The conspiracy is theirs, not mine. They have bribed your Goddess, flattered her and lied to her, coerced her all-powerful goodness to their own evil interests, preparing for the day when they could persuade her to cast your land into the fiery furnace of a ten-year-drought—"

Somebody in the middle of the court burst out laughing. One by one the natives nudged one another, and booed, and guffawed, until the rising tide of racket drowned out Zeckler's words. "The defendant is obviously lying," roared the prosecutor over the pandemonium. "Any fool knows that the Goddess can't be bribed. How could she be a Goddess if she could?"

Zeckler grew paler. "But—perhaps they were very clever—"

"And how could they flatter her, when she knows, beyond doubt, that she is the most exquisitely radiant creature in all the Universe? And *you* dare to insult her, drag her name in the dirt."

The hisses grew louder, more belligerent. Cries of "Butcher

him!" and "Scald his bowels!" rose from the courtroom. The judge banged for silence, his eyes angry.

"Unless the defendant wishes to take up more of our precious time with these ridiculous lies, the jury—"

"Wait! Your Honor, I request a short recess before I present my final plea."

"Recess?"

"A few moments to collect my thoughts, to arrange my case."

The judge settled back with a disgusted snarl. "Do I have to?" he asked Meyerhoff.

Meyerhoff nodded. The judge shrugged, pointing over his shoulder to the anteroom. "You can go in there," he said.

Somehow, Zeckler managed to stumble from the witness stand, amid riotous boos and hisses, and tottered into the anteroom.

Zeckler puffed hungrily on a cigarette, and looked up at Meyerhoff with haunted eyes. "It—it doesn't look so good," he muttered.

Meyerhoff's eyes were worried, too. For some reason, he felt a surge of pity and admiration for the haggard con-man. "It's worse than I'd anticipated," he admitted glumly. "That was a good try, but you just don't know enough about them and their Goddess." He sat down wearily. "I don't see what you can do. They want your blood, and they're going to have it. They just won't believe you, no matter *how* big a lie you tell."

Zeckler sat in silence for a moment. "This lying business," he said finally, "exactly how does it work?"

"The biggest, most convincing liar wins. It's as simple as that. It doesn't matter how outlandish a whopper you tell.

Unless, of course, they've made up their minds that you just naturally aren't as big a liar as they are. And it looks like that's just what they've done. It wouldn't make any difference to them *what* you say—unless, somehow, you could *make* them believe it."

Zeckler frowned. "And how do they regard the—the biggest liar? I mean, how do they feel toward him?"

Meyerhoff shifted uneasily. "It's hard to say. It's been my experience that they respect him highly—maybe even fear him a little. After all, the most convincing liar always wins in any transaction, so he gets more land, more food, more power. Yes, I think the biggest liar could go where he pleased without any interference."

Zeckler was on his feet, his eyes suddenly bright with excitement. "Wait a minute," he said tensely. "To tell them a lie that they'd have to believe—a lie they simply couldn't *help* but believe—" He turned on Meyerhoff, his hands trembling. "Do they *think* the way we do? I mean, with logic, cause and effect, examining evidence and drawing conclusions? Given certain evidence, would they have to draw the same conclusions that we have to draw?"

Meyerhoff blinked. "Well—yes. Oh, yes, they're perfectly logical."

Zeckler's eyes flashed, and a huge grin broke out on his sallow face. His thin body fairly shook. He started hopping up and down on one foot, staring idiotically into space. "If I could only think—" he muttered. "Somebody—somewhere—something I read."

"Whatever are you talking about?"

"It was a Greek, I think—"

Meyerhoff stared at him. "Oh, come now. Have you gone

off your rocker completely? You've got a problem on your hands, man."

"No, no, I've got a problem in the bag!" Zeckler's cheeks flushed. "Let's go back in there—I think I've got an answer!"

The courtroom quieted the moment they opened the door, and the judged banged the gavel for silence. As soon as Zeckler had taken his seat on the witness stand, the judge turned to the head juryman. "Now, then," he said with happy finality. "The jury—"

"Hold on! Just one minute more."

The judge stared down at Zeckler as if he were a bug on a rock. "Oh, yes. You had something else to say. Well, go ahead and say it."

Zeckler looked sharply around the hushed room. "You want to convict me," he said softly, "in the worst sort of way. Isn't that right?"

Eyes swung toward him. The judge broke into an evil grin. "That's right."

"But you can't really convict me until you've considered carefully any statement I make in my own defense. Isn't that right?"

The judge looked uncomfortable. "If you've got something to say, go ahead and say it."

"I've got just one statement to make. Short and sweet. But you'd better listen to it, and think it out carefully before you decide that you really want to convict me." He paused, and glanced slyly at the judge. "You don't think much of those who tell the truth, it seems. Well, put *this* statement in your record, then," His voice was loud and clear in the still room. "*All Earthmen are absolutely incapable of telling the truth.*"

Puzzled frowns appeared on the jury's faces. One or two exchanged startled glances, and the room was still as death.

The judge stared at him, and then at Meyerhoff, then back. "But you"—he stammered. "You're"—He stopped in mid-sentence, his jaw sagging.

One of the jurymen let out a little squeak, and fainted dead away. It took, all in all, about ten seconds for the statement to soak in.

And then pandemonium broke loose in the courtroom.

"Really," said Harry Zeckler loftily, "it was so obvious I'm amazed that it didn't occur to me first thing." He settled himself down comfortably in the control cabin of the Interplanetary Rocket and grinned at the outline of Altair IV looming larger in the view screen.

Paul Meyerhoff stared stonily at the controls, his lips compressed angrily. "You might at least have told me what you were planning."

"And take the chance of being overheard? Don't be silly. It had to come as a bombshell. I had to establish myself as a liar—the prize liar of them all, but I had to tell the sort of lie that they simply could not cope with. Something that would throw them into such utter confusion that they wouldn't *dare* convict me." He grinned impishly at Meyerhoff. "The paradox of Epiminedes the Cretan. It really stopped them cold. They *knew* I was an Earthmen, which meant that my statement that Earthmen were liars was a lie, which meant that maybe I wasn't a liar, in which case—oh, it was tailor-made."

"It sure was." Meyerhoff's voice was a snarl.

"Well, it made me out a liar in a class they couldn't approach, didn't it?"

Meyerhoff's face was purple with anger. "Oh, indeed it did! And it put *all* Earthmen in exactly the same class, too."

"So what's honor among thieves? I got off, didn't I?"

Meyerhoff turned on him fiercely. "Oh, you got off just fine. You scared the living daylights out of them. And in an eon of lying they never have run up against a short-circuit like that. You've also completely botched any hope of ever setting up a trading alliance with Altair I, and that includes uranium, too. Smart people don't gamble with loaded dice. You scared them so badly they don't want anything to do with us."

Zeckler's grin broadened, and he leaned back luxuriously. "Ah, well. After all, the Trading Alliance was *your* outlook, wasn't it? What a pity!" He clucked his tongue sadly. "Me, I've got a fortune in credits sitting back at the consulate waiting for me—enough to keep me on silk for quite a while, I might say. I think I'll just take a nice, long vacation."

Meyerhoff turned to him, and a twinkle of malignant glee appeared in his eyes. "Yes, I think you will. I'm quite sure of it, in fact. Won't cost you a cent, either."

"Eh?"

Meyerhoff grinned unpleasantly. He brushed an imaginary lint fleck from his lapel, and looked up at Zeckler slyly. "That —uh—jury trial. The Altairians weren't any too happy to oblige. They wanted to execute you outright. Thought a trial was awfully silly—until they got their money back, of course." Not too much—just three million credits."

Zeckler went white. "But that money was in banking custody!"

"Is that right? My goodness. You don't suppose they could have lost those papers, do you?" Meyerhoff grinned at the little con-man. "And incidentally, you're under arrest, you know."

A choking sound came from Zeckler's throat. "*Arrest!*"

"Oh, yes. Didn't I tell you? Conspiring to undermine the authority of the Terran Trading Commission. Serious charge, you know. Yes, I think we'll take a nice long vacation together, straight back to Terra. And there I think you'll face a jury trial."

Zeckler spluttered. "There's no evidence—you've got nothing on me! What kind of a frame are you trying to pull?"

"A *lovely* frame. Airtight. A frame from the bottom up, and you're right square in the middle. And this time—" Meyerhoff tapped a cigarette on his thumb with happy finality—"this time I *don't* think you'll get off."

Family Resemblance

IT really started off as a prank, as so many things do, and it would have remained a prank if Dr. Herman Tally hadn't happened into the hospital nursery at precisely the moment he did—or if he hadn't had a fight with Dr. Hogan just before, which left his mind a fertile field for mischief. And there wouldn't even have *been* a prank if it hadn't been Tuesday, and if Miss Henderson in the nursery had been less inclined to squeal when excited.

But it *was* Tuesday, in the early summer, when the life of a hospital intern became dull and many a fledgling doctor, like Dr. Barret, for instance, was itching for excitement to relieve the humdrum routine of patients and case histories. The hospital cook was also partly to blame, for the three doctors were sitting about the interns' table at St. Christopher's Hospital that day, eating the inevitable Tuesday fare of pigs-in-a-blanket and sauerkraut, and wondering how to break the monotony.

"What," said Dr. Barret as he stared at his dinner plate, "makes more noise than a pig under a gate?"

"Two pigs," muttered Dr. Hines, munching thoughtfully. "Or three pigs under a blanket. You're out of date."

"Oh, no," smiled Dr. Barret, the faintest gleam in his young hazel eyes. "For your information the answer is: Miss Henderson, when she's suffered an emotional shock!"

Miss Henderson, the newest proby nurse at St. Christopher's, was at present assigned to uneasy duty with Dr. Barret in the maternity ward, and had suffered numerous emotional shocks, it seemed, under that gentleman's tender care. Miss Henderson was, as they put it, a lush dish; she was also a trifle gullible.

Dr. Barret chuckled in unashamed malice. "You should have heard her," he grinned, "when she spotted that wiggly green lizard jiggling down my jacket front the other day. She squealed like five pigs under a gate!" The doctors laughed and leaned closer to Dr. Barret, sensing a scheme under construction. "Now, Miss Henderson is in the nursery this afternoon," he speculated softly. "What do you suppose she would do if she found . . ."

It was very simple to arrange. Dr. Barret took a quick trip across the campus to the Agricultural Experiment Station after lunch and returned to the hospital as unobtrusively as possible through a rear entrance, hoping that none of the staff doctors would notice the odd bulge under his intern's jacket. Five minutes later he exhibited his prize to his fellow conspirators in their rooms, where they scrubbed it with soap and water and sprinkled it liberally with baby powder, amid much outraged squealing, until the barest whiff of ether settled it down into a snuffling and uneasy sleep. Then the other two interns waylaid Miss Henderson, giggling and self-conscious, in the chart room while Dr. Barret placed the prize in a baby basket in the nursery, neatly wrapping it in a blue baby blanket and arranging it between the basket tagged "Child Harrison" and the one labeled "Child Wojikowsky." He left it there with a small but distinctly legible tag at the bottom of the basket: "Child Porker."

The three were watching from the nursery door, maintaining a studied and valiant calm, when Miss Henderson, still giggling and meditating future dates with handsome doctors, marched into the nursery with the two-o'clock bottles for Child Harrison and Child Wojikowsky. Her reaction was gratifying indeed. She stopped in her tracks, let out the prize squeal of her eighteen years, and fainted dead away.

It might have remained only a prank if just at that moment Dr. Herman Tally, Professor of Anthropology, student of infant development, and chief whipping boy of Dr. Hogan's anthropological research staff, had not arrived to make his weekly rounds of St. Christopher's nursery. Dr. Tally was essentially a mild man, calmly gratified if his daily routine was allowed to run its course without too many ragged edges, from rising in the morning to retiring at night. He was certainly *not* mentally prepared for three startled interns, a bewildered nurse, and the apparition in the baby basket as he climbed the nursery stairs that afternoon.

He was muttering to himself at the most recent indignities suffered at the hands of his chief. The lazy pig! It wasn't enough that Dr. Hogan required him to type, rewrite, proofread, index, and play public relations supervisor for the Book—he had to collect the man's research data for him, too, when Dr. Hogan didn't feel like hoisting his porcine bulk down to St. Christopher's nursery on a hot Tuesday afternoon. Dr. Tally sighed tiredly. For three years now the Book had occupied the entire working hours of the whole anthropology staff.

"Back to the Apes," Dr. Hogan would beam, expounding enthusiastically, "will be the last word on the Origin of Man conflict—the *last word,* I say, the crowning blow to all opposing theories!" He would puff and wheeze in excitement. Then,

smiling his fat smile upon anyone who was still listening: "My final work will be published in *Back to the Apes,* proving, I say *proving* that man and ape alike look back on a common ancestor!" And then Dr. Hogan would beam some more.

Dr. Tally grimaced. He was so tired of going back to the apes. The title wasn't even Dr. Hogan's idea, and some of the harebrained ideas that *were* his, like these recent tests on infant reactions—Dr. Tally reached the top of the stairs, enveloped in gloom, and walked into the nursery.

Miss Henderson was already enjoying the solicitous attention of the three young interns, so Dr. Tally looked immediately for the cause of her sudden collapse. The sight of the baby basket took him quite aback. For a moment he stared at it in disbelief, until in a flash of insight he recognized all the earmarks of an intern's sense of humor. Nevertheless, he still stared at the basket. And stared, and stared.

Then the idea exploded in his mind, almost frightening him. Something there struck a chord, a beautiful harmony, far back in his memory. Some resemblance to something he had seen, or read—he ran a trembling hand through his sparse hair as he thought, probing the vast store of incidental and disorganized material in his mind. There had been so much to learn in anatomy, or physiology—or was it embryology? The more he stared at Child Porker, snuffling in its basket, the stronger the idea became, forcing itself into his mind, carrying him closer and closer to the familiar link.

Embryology! *That* was it! Dr. Tally jammed his hat on his head and beat a hasty retreat down the stairs. Embryology! In the back of his mind, he knew there was something about embryology. If he could only find the book. . . .

Dr. Tally was late for supper, and when he came up the walk from his battered Chevy, arms loaded with books, he viewed dinner with a certain degree of abstraction. It had been embryology indeed, and much, more more. The afternoon had been spent in the library stacks, checking first one embryology test and then another. It was after an hour there that he grew certain he had a trail to follow, but a complex trail, with many devious twistings. It took him into anatomy, into physiology, into biochemistry. He kissed his wife, hardly seeing her, and settled down to his belated supper, opening Benson's *Parasitology* on one side of his plate and Best and Taylor's *Physiological Basis for Medical Practice* on the other side. In a matter of moments he was immersed, his thin shoulders trembling with agitation.

"Dear," said Mrs. Tally, hopefully, "are you enjoying your chops? They're very expensive nowadays."

"Chops?"

"Pork chops. What you're eating. Aren't they delicious?"

He looked up from his books, first at his wife, then at the chops, his face slightly green. "My dear," he said, pushing his plate away gently but with finality, "I'm afraid I just can't enjoy the . . . dinner . . . this evening. I've a great deal of work to do, and I'd like to be undisturbed tonight." He rose unsteadily from the table, books under his arm, and retreated into his study.

The trail was unmistakable, clear and distinct. For years people had nodded sagely and accepted authority unchallenged, even when they had crossed the trail in a dozen places. It was here, winding its way through a dozen books, never examined, never correlated, but here! Anyone with half an eye could find it. They had just missed it because they hadn't dared to look. And all the palaver about scientific method! He pored over the *Parasitology*, then checked several chapters of human physiology. Darwin's *Origin of the Species* came next, then the embryology text again and a huge volume on dental surgery. Three large tomes on psychological conditioning and reflex reactions occupied him for almost an hour before he tossed them aside with a sigh and sought out a chapter on human nasal surgery. All here, all so clear, and nobody had thought to make the necessary correlation! His heart was in his throat, his whole mind afire with the expanse of his vision when his wife brought in a sandwich and milk, well past midnight. She saw a gleam in her husband's eye that she hadn't seen in ten years under Dr. Hogan's tyranny.

"Darling," said Dr. Tally, after munching for a while on the sandwich, "how would you like to go away for a while—take an extended vacation, for instance?"

"Go away?" She looked up in surprise. "Why, Herman! We haven't been on a vacation in ten years! Where to?"

A faraway look came into the doctor's eyes. "Some beautiful island, maybe in the South Pacific. Maybe we could go to New Zealand, or Central Africa. I hear they need anthropologists in Central Africa."

Her eyes were wide, and she brushed back her graying hair with studied care. "Herman, you aren't yourself tonight. What's wrong? Are you in trouble?"

He stood up, swelling his thin chest with air. "The biggest trouble in ten years, my dear, and the most wonderful! I've discovered something that's likely to lose me my job so fast I won't know what hit me!"

"Something that will oppose Dr. Hogan?"

"Oppose him! It'll knock him and his theories right out the door. And it'll get me fired on the spot. The Board of Trustees may throw me out on my ear, if I can't convince them, but I'm going to do it if they put me on a spit and roast me! The great Dr. Hogan has been rooting in my cornfield for years, and now I've got a stick big enough to drive him out!"

Dr. Horace Hogan's office was the largest, brightest, best-equipped office-lab in the Zoology Building. His first book, *The Essence of the Ape,* had given him the laboratory and the prestige and the power over his subordinates, as well as altogether too much to eat in the past five years or so. He hoisted his blubbery bulk around in the swivel chair to face Dr. Tally, his fat face heavy with annoyance.

"Yes, yes, Dr. Tally, what is it? You know I'm not to be disturbed when I'm writing."

"Dr. Hogan, I have a question to ask you." Dr. Tally's face was drawn tight, a cold light of determination in his eyes. He wondered, abstractedly, how Dr. Hogan would look roasted, with an apple in his mouth.

"Well, you'll have to see me later. *Back to the Apes* comes first in this office, you know. I've a deadline to make."

"Bother the deadline," said Dr. Tally succinctly. "You won't need to make it. And I want my question answered here"—he drew himself up straight and proud—"and now!"

The fat man spluttered and swung back to face him. "All right," he said testily. "Out with it, man. What's the trouble?"

"What is the complete biological classification of man?"

Dr. Hogan's face went blank with surprise. "Chordata, Craniata, Mammalia, Primata, Hominidae, Homo sapiens," he snapped mechanically. "Our freshman premedics were asked that question on their first-hour quiz, Dr. Tally."

"Yes," said Dr. Tally softly. "I suppose they were also asked to trace the human evolutionary chain back to a common ancestor with the apes, weren't they?"

"Of course they were! That is undoubtedly the most precious

and fundamental single item of knowledge they will ever have occasion to encounter!" The fat man quivered, his face red.

Dr. Tally smiled. "But if they give *your* answer, they might all be wrong!"

"Dr. Tally!" Dr. Hogan started to his feet, thought better of it, and assumed a pose of militant indignation from a sitting position. "Such a remark is heresy, Dr. Tally. Heresy!"

Dr. Tally pulled a sheaf of papers from his briefcase. "Listen to me for a moment, Dr. Hogan, and correct me if I'm wrong. In tracing the evolutionary line of any creature, we look to generalized rather than specialized forms, isn't that right? And for that reason we consider man from the point of view of the biological family, Hominidae, rather than the specialized genus and species, Homo sapiens."

"That's right."

"And we look to the ancestral form with similar generalized characteristics when we want to find the progenitor of man?"

"Of course. You know that."

"And you are entirely satisfied that man's evolutionary chain sprang from the family Tarsius, now represented by certain monkeys and apes?"

Dr. Hogan wheezed in agitation. "For the dignity of man, I am inalterably convinced, Dr. Tally. 'Back to the apes,' I always say. All the evidence points—"

"Not *all* the evidence, Dr. Hogan! The evidence found in anthropology, perhaps, and paleontology. But there are other lines of evidence, modern evidence, unmistakable evidence. You can't twist scientific methods around a pole to suit your whims! There is evidence that does not point to Tarsius or the apes at all. It points directly and unmistakably to the Suidae!"

Dr. Hogan gasped, his hog-like jowls bobbing up and down.

"Preposterous!" he gasped. "Of course, there may be certain faint resemblance, but to relate human beings, *human beings,* mind you, to *pigs!*"

Dr. Tally grinned a wicked grin. "There certainly are resemblances. Your evidence for the apes is anthropological, paleontological, but I have anatomical, physiological and embryological evidence." He settled down in a chair. "Look at the evidence, Dr. Hogan. I remembered, from back in my college days, that somebody had once remarked, during an embryology course, that we studied the embryos of pigs rather than human beings because they were more easily available and *essentially the same!* I checked it. They are indubitably the same, Dr. Hogan, in almost every way. Only in the last few weeks of gestation does a pig embryo become distinguishable from a human embryo. And after birth, what anatomical relation is there? The organs, the viscera, the internal arrangement of the pig is *practically identical* with that of man! The same size, placement, shape, function for all the organs. The apes present a very different anatomical picture. Both men and pigs have similar vermiform appendixes—apes do not. Human teeth have either one root or two in the premolars and molars, while in monkeys and apes these same teeth have three roots. In pigs these teeth are rooted the same as in man. And other things—men and pigs have little or no vestigial tails, while apes and monkeys have either short or long tails. Men and pigs are essentially hairless; monkeys and apes, even up to the gorillas, all have hair in abundance—"

Dr. Hogan's face was turning a dangerous vermilion hue, his eyes bulging from their sockets. "Superficialities!" he hissed, wiping his forehead with a pudgy hand. "Of all the impertinent, disgraceful ideas—"

"But there are other 'superficialities,'" Dr. Tally cut in.

"Pigs and men have cartilage all around their noses, while monkeys and apes have slit noses. Pigs and men have that odd bit of useless tissue, the uvula, tacked on to the back of their palates, while there is little or no uvula among monkeys and apes. Are these superficialities? Doesn't science demand attention to little things?"

"Preposterous!" sputtered Dr. Hogan.

"Oh, I'm not finished! Let's go a little deeper. How about parasites? Ever hear of Trichina? Or Macracanthorynchus, and other hook-headed worms? What mammalian forms do these parasites attack? Man and pig, but never apes and monkeys. How about serological comparisons, blood serum and cells, and the like? Man is at least as close serologically to pigs as he is to apes. Oh, I could go on for hours, Dr. Hogan, but there's one comparison that puts the clincher on the whole thing. We've talked about paleontology and anatomy and physiology—how about psychology?"

"Well, *what* about psychology?" roared Dr. Hogan, his whole body trembling.

Dr. Tally smiled. "Why do you suppose pigs are used for conditioning experiments now, in preference to rats and dogs and cats? *Because they react more like man.* The pig stands far above cats and dogs and rats and many monkeys in the intelligence scale. And what other animal, Dr. Hogan, besides man, is so consistently lazy, gluttonous, dirty, selfish, treacherous, or pugnacious?"

By now Dr. Hogan was quivering wtih rage, his round, fat face damp with small beads of perspiration. "You . . . you'd never dare to publish such a thing!" he said in a hoarse whisper. "What would it do to our culture? What would people think, what would they say? They'd never believe it or accept it. We'd have to rearrange our entire thinking processes, our philospohical values. It would throw the world into chaos, Dr. Tally. Why, you'd have almost every religious group in the country down on our necks."

Dr. Tally was smiling. "And I might, just possibly, make people wonder if Horace Hogan isn't just a bit of a goat with his 'back to the apes' theory, mightn't I?"

Dr. Hogan tried to keep his voice from squeaking. "Now, Herman, consider!" he said. "Why, we've been friends for years, associates in our work, almost brothers, you might say." He wheezed a bit and his little pig eyes watched Tally shrewdly. "I know you wouldn't want to discredit me, who has done so much for you, and I *know* you wouldn't want to start any such storm as this. Now, if you wish, we might arrange an associate professorship, and see that you got a substantial raise in salary."

Dr. Tally shook his head, grinning widely. "There's something I'd much rather do," he said. "I'd rather see Horace Hogan grow thin—with worry, perhaps. You can't bribe me or talk me out of it, Horace. I'm going to put the skids under that book of yours."

This time the fat man did hoist himself out of his seat, his face deep purple. "Traitor!" he screamed. "Ingrate! Get out! You're fired! Get out! Do your worst! But you won't get anywhere. The Board of Trustees will throw you out on your ear, and you'll be the laughing-stock of the scholarly world. Pigs, indeed!" Frantically he fumbled for a telephone. "I'll call the board right now, and you'll be through."

Dr. Tally coughed gently. "Dr. Hogan, you won't have to call the board. As a matter of fact, they're waiting out in the office right now. I've already told them, you see, and they're—interested. Yes, you might say they're interested, and I've taken the liberty to arrange a little tour for them. Over at St. Christopher's Hospital."

They were five elderly gentlemen. All five were tall, and all were lean, with narrow hawk noses and stooped shoulders and sharp blue eyes peering disapprovingly at Dr. Horace Hogan as they made their way up the stairs to the hospital nursery. Dr. Hogan waddled ahead of them, panting and spluttering for all the world like an angry old sow routed from her wallow. His pudgy face was damp, and his hands trembled as he worked his way up the steps, stopping periodically to pant a few spluttered words of protest. "Pigs! Can you imagine, gentlemen, the temerity of this man?"

"Yes, yes, Dr. Hogan, but if, as he says, there is some reason to believe—"

"Preposterous! My work has been most scientific, there have been no loopholes. All the important evidence points—"

One of the elderly gentlemen looked down his lean nose at Dr. Hogan. "But surely a man with your acquaintance with scientific methods should be willing at least to listen to an hypothesis!"

Dr. Tally sprinted up the stairs ahead of them, his face pale, lines of worry on his forehead. At the top of the stairs he showed the men to seats in the anteroom. "If you'll just be seated, gentlemen, I'll check to make sure we aren't disturbing feeding—" He disappeared through a white-painted door, and almost collided with Dr. Barret.

The intern looked up, and grabbed at Dr. Tally's sleeve nervously. "Look, Doc, that's the Board of Trustees out there! They hire and fire around here! You didn't tell me it would be *them* when you called this morning. You just said some old fogies."

Dr. Tally nodded his head vigorously. "You've got everything arranged?"

The intern looked worriedly over his shoulder. "Sure, everything's just like you said, but you'll never get away with it."

"I've *got* to get away with it! I've planted the seed in fertile minds, and they'll see what they want to see. And particularly, they'll see Horace Hogan—" He patted the intern nervously on the arm and hurried back to the waiting room. "Now, gentlemen, if you'll just come with me."

Slowly they walked through the door and down the darkened corridor, past the viewing windows, to the very last room. The five members of the board and Dr. Hogan filed up to the window and looked in, and silence fell abruptly over the party.

Inside, a subdued Miss Henderson moved efficiently from basket to basket, gently turning back the pink and blue blankets.

"What—"

"Impossible! Why, if I didn't see it with my own eyes—"

"There *is* a resemblance! Unmistakable! Why, how could this have been missed all these years? Dr. Tally, this is the most remarkable—"

Suddenly in the corridor there was a choked roar of anguish and despair, ending in a little gurgle and a heavy thud. This time Dr. Hogan fainted dead away. The elderly men looked around in alarm as several solicitous interns appeared, to ease Hogan's bulk onto a stretcher and start resuscitating him. Dr. Tally herded his charges gently out into the bright light of the anteroom once again.

"Basically unstable," he whispered, jerking his thumb over his shoulder. "Couldn't bear to have his ideas refuted. But I'm sure you can see, gentlemen, that here is something worthy of careful investigation."

The five elderly men looked at one another, and back at Dr. Tally, and suddenly there appeared five broad and understanding smiles. "Yes, Dr. Tally. We're quite sure."

"What I can't see," said Dr. Barret later, as Dr. Tally helped him lug the heavy, squealing crates back toward the Agricultural Experiment Station, "is how you can reconcile this sort of thing with the 'scientfic method' you're always yapping about. So maybe men came from pigs—it seems quite possible—but this is a funny way to prove it."

"Oh, it's *quite* possible. But this wasn't supposed to prove anything at all, really. Merely to give me a chance to try. We won't be bothered by Dr. Hogan and his wretched book any more." Dr. Tally turned twinkling eyes toward the young intern. "Though I'm afraid my methods of convincing would have insulted one of the greatest minds man has ever turned out—the very father of the scientific method."

Dr. Barret looked up sharply. "You mean—"

Dr. Tally nodded apologetically. "Roger Bacon," he said.